TIME SCHOOL

We Will Remember Them

Nikki Young

STORYMAKERS PRESS

First published in Great Britain by Troubador Publishing 2018
This edition published in Great Britain by Storymakers Press 2021

Text copyright © Nicola Young 2021
Copyright Cover illustration © Tim Budgen 2020
Cover Design © Helen Braid 2020

A CIP catalogue for this book is available from the British Library.

ISBN 978-1-8384687-0-5

Typeset in Garamond Classic 11.75/14.5 by Blaze Typesetting

Storymakers Press
Kent, England, United Kingdom
Website: www.storymakersclub.com

To my family

Acknowledgements

When I was a little girl, I wanted to be a journalist. More specifically, I wanted to write features for a magazine. It may come as a surprise, therefore, to know that I ended up studying sciences and maths - by the time I got to A-Levels, I was forcibly guided into the science route against my better judgement, but pitched up against adults who seemed to think they knew what was best for me. Despite this, I somehow always managed to steer whatever job I had towards something writing related - at my very first job, I had a feature published on food allergies and intolerances. Writing was always where I felt most comfortable.

As cliché as it sounds, I have, for as long as I can remember, wanted to be an author. The problem was, I didn't know what I wanted to write about. That was, until I became a mum and began to experience my children's journey to reading. It was then I remembered how important reading had been to me as a child, when I spent most weeks at Heckmondwike library with my mum, devouring everything in the children's section. I don't remember ever having brand new books but it never stopped me reading. I spent hours at the top of a Swiss mountain, countless days in the creeks of the American West wilderness and umpteen adventures in an idyllic English countryside. None of these places resembled the tired old Victorian market town where I grew up. That didn't seem to matter though. These surroundings have still influenced my own writing.

The remnants of the glory days of the Victorian

industrial revolution are still visible in my home town, though you have to look hard to see them. The mills that once churned out the wool that carpeted and clothed the Empire are long gone, turned into flats and shopping complexes. The many railway lines that served the area now lie disused, overgrown and reclaimed by the land. What remains is the legacy of the architects of that time, the library being one of them, my old school, the other. So much change has occurred around those buildings. The economic decline of the area, socio-economic and political change, historical events, all while these buildings have steadfastly remained in silent observation. It occurred to me one day that my old school, Heckmondwike Grammar, had continued educating young people regardless of what was going on around it. It was the one constant among a sea of so much change and I began to explore that idea for my Time School series. The towns of Hickley and Kirkshaw from the books are loosely based on Heckmondwike and nearby Dewsbury, though none of the characters are based on real life people and many of the features in the books are made up - there is no railway line between the two towns, for example, even though there once would have been.

I have my husband to thank for encouraging me to write. He believed in me even when I so often didn't believe in myself. Also, becoming a mum reawakened me to the true joy of discovering great stories, making me realise what sort of writer I wanted to be. Reading was my saviour as a child and I truly believe in its importance. To be even just a small part of that brings me great joy.

My children, Hope, Scarlett and Ike are my biggest

critics, as well as my greatest allies. I cannot write this acknowledgement without thanking them for their patience and for letting me read numerous drafts of this story to them. The book itself, wouldn't be where it is without my editor, Vicky Blunden, though. It is always a joy, and a relief, to work with an editor who gets you, understands your work and genuinely loves the characters as much as you do. There have been occasions when I might have given up if it weren't for my writing buddies, Maddy, Renee, Alice, Jo, Chrissie, Teika, Sophie, Antonia, Becky, Sarah, Rachael, encouraging me on. As one put it, being with these ladies is soul strengthening and I couldn't agree more. Also, thanks to Linden for all your support and for having me as a guest on your monthly Bookclub on BBC Radio Kent.

My creative imagination, not dampened by the sciences, has my oldest and dearest friend, Chloe, to thank. As the childhood heroines of our youth, we are kindred spirits, who grew up sharing a love of stories that is as strong as our bond, no matter how far from each other we are. Thanks must also go to all the parents who bring their children to my Storymakers Writing Club, which leads on nicely to the children who come to my weekly groups and workshops. I know you've been waiting for this, so I hope it doesn't disappoint!

Chapter 1

The Ghosts Within These Walls

"Has anyone ever asked where you come from? Do you know? Mr Mundair?"

"Yes, Miss. I came from Kirkshaw this morning."

Ash Mundair. Already firmly established as the class joker within the first few weeks of the Year Sevens beginning their secondary school careers. There was a collective giggle that spread across the room like air escaping from an untied balloon. Mrs Kennedy, the history teacher, remained straight-faced. She'd seen it all, and worse, before.

"Thank you for that, Ash, but you know what I'm talking about—your family tree. Your roots and please, no mention of grey hairs and hair dye."

The class giggled once more as Ash pulled at his spiky black hair. His face one that expressed pure innocence but for the sparkle in his dark eyes made large and round by the glasses that framed them.

"We all have rich histories, more interesting than you might think and our heritage connects us to the area in which we live and the changes that have happened during that time," Mrs Kennedy explained. "Think about this school. In one hundred and twenty years, it's seen a lot of changes, not only physically, as buildings have been added, but culturally, economically and politically too. This classroom we're in right now, and the hall just through that door, are part of the original building of this school. You're sitting in a lesson, just as hundreds of children have done before you. Imagine if these four walls could talk and what they would say about the things they've seen and heard over the years. The ghosts of the past are absorbed within the walls of this building and as part of our history project this term, we're going to explore that."

There was nothing in the classroom to indicate it was anything other than bland and uninteresting. The stale smell of sweat in the air, punctuated with cheap body spray and anticipation, reminding you it was a room full of pre-teens, sitting restlessly on plastic chairs designed to be as uncomfortable as possible. Double desks lined the room, all facing a whiteboard, names scratched into the surface, gum stuck hard underneath.

Jess Chadwick sat up straight. Was that what Mrs Kennedy meant by the ghosts of the past being with them? Had other children sat in this very room, staring at the peeling white paint of the huge sash windows that looked out on to the road beyond, with nothing but an old work unit for a view? Grey on grey, obscured by cobwebs and dust. Minds filled with anything other than what the teacher had to say.

Although she didn't hate it, school was a place where you had to go, day in, day out, until finally the day came when you didn't have to go anymore. It was a constant in your life, as sure as the sun rising in the morning and setting at night.

Jess wondered if that's how pupils of the past had thought of it. Had they enjoyed learning, or dreaded the whole idea? Stressed about exams, or relished the thought of being in a classroom rather than working for a living?

A few weeks into the start of Year Seven and Jess was beginning to settle into the routine of secondary school. The thought of moving on from her small, safe junior school had made her anxious. She wasn't like her best friends Nadia, Tomma and Ash. They were full of confidence and ready to move on. Jess would have stayed at her old school forever if they'd have let her. The only comfort had been knowing she was moving on with the three friends she'd been inseparable from for as long as she could remember. It had been a huge relief when they'd all been put in the same class as well—something that helped ease the anxiety of the change.

Hickley School had felt enormous to begin with. Flanked on all four sides by roads and housing, it wasn't that big for a secondary school. It was a mixed bag of buildings, added on over the years, using all of the available space. But with everyone so cramped together, it felt like there were thousands of pupils, making for a hectic and noisy environment that had initially seemed intimidating.

As a newcomer, Jess felt small, young and immature. The older years looked down on them as the babies, which was embarrassing, to say the least. Jess was almost twelve! She didn't feel like a baby and didn't want to be treated like one. So far, she'd stuck close to her friends and avoided eye contact with anyone who wasn't in her year group.

"Double History to start the day. Bo-oring," Ash said.

It was break time and they were perched on a low wall in the yard reserved for Year Sevens only. Jess took the opportunity to look around. She hadn't appreciated that the entrance hub just across from them was a modern glass bubble added on to what was the original school building. The sand-coloured Yorkshire stone walls were discoloured from the pollution of time, like many of the buildings of Hickley town and the surrounding area—remnants of its Victorian industrial past, when the mills churned out wool that made cloth and carpets, exported across the Empire. When coal mines fuelled the mills, and the steam trains that transported the goods. All that remained of those prosperous days were disused rail tracks and falling down old mills.

Here, at the school, however, the past came together with the present in a way that didn't make sense, but somehow worked, showing how the school had evolved. It was a sign of its strength, rather than of any weakness.

Whereas the town around it had somehow lost its identity along the way and was struggling to understand its place in the world, Hickley School was stronger than ever. The number of times Jess had been reminded of how lucky she was to have a place there was a testament to that.

"At least you actually have an interesting history," Jess said, looking at Ash, who was balancing on the wall on one leg.

Reminded on a daily basis of where he came from and how lucky he was, Ash was more than aware of his heritage. His dad's struggles as a young Indian boy coming over to England from Uganda in the 1970s were held around Ash's neck like a noose, constantly pressing down upon him. As far as his dad was concerned, what was the point in going through all that, if his own children weren't going to work hard and make a better life for themselves? To Ash, it was like an annoying song stuck on repeat. He liked to have fun and messing about at school was his speciality. Despite the pressures from home, Ash refused to take life too seriously.

Jess had lived her whole life in nearby Kirkshaw village, in the same house with her mum, dad and older brother, Declan: standard family, ordinary life. . . dull.

"As far as I know, my family's from Kirkshaw and there's nothing remotely exciting or interesting about my history," she said. "I'm not part Polish like Nadia, or half Croatian, like Tomma. Just out and out Yorkshire."

"Like the Brontë's," said Nadia. "Nothing wrong with that."

"Not exactly exciting though, is it?" Jess said.

"There's nothing exciting about my life either," Nadia said. "The only Polish part of me is my name."

"Or mine," Tomma said. "I've never even been to Croatia and Mum never talks about it. It's like that part of her life never existed."

"Have you ever asked?" Jess said.

"Yeah, course! But she gets all weird, so it's best not to," he said.

One side of Tomma's mouth looped up in a half-smile-half-frown, but his almond-shaped eyes betrayed a concern the rest of his face tried to hide. Only Jess could see that. She knew Tomma almost as well as she knew herself.

"You know, Jess, that red hair of yours has to come from somewhere," Ash said. "You never know. You might be Irish or Scottish down the line."

Jess's hand immediately flew to her hair, tied low in a side plait. She'd always been slightly embarrassed by it, worried she'd be teased for being ginger. Most people only gave compliments though, about what a gorgeous colour it was. She was yet to decide whether she agreed with them on that.

She wished she had Tomma's or Nadia's darker skin tone. Her skin was easily burnt and erupted in freckles at the slightest touch of the sun's rays. She smiled, despite her reservations about her looks. Perhaps it might be interesting to delve more deeply into her past. Maybe she would uncover something that would make her life seem as interesting as those of her best friends? Despite what they said, Jess knew instinctively that Nadia, Tomma and Ash would uncover far more about their past histories than she ever could.

Chapter 2

Power Failure

Jess woke to the sound of shouting and banging from downstairs. In her dazed state, she realised her alarm hadn't gone off and for a brief moment, had trouble working out what day it was.

Peeling herself from under the cosy warmth of her duvet, Jess peered out of her bedroom door, with all the caution you'd expect from someone who had just woken up, eyes not yet focused. The scene before her was like a video in fast-forward as her older brother, Declan, ran past her towards the bathroom.

"Clocks stopped. Power cut. All late," he said, before slamming the door shut, making Jess jump.

Jess shook her head in irritation. Declan had an annoying habit of talking in clipped tones, never seeming to feel the need to use full sentences. It was only a matter of time before he added words like 'Hashtag' to his speech.

She stood for a few seconds, letting his words seep into her sleepy brain before turning around and looking at the powder blue, digital radio alarm clock on the chest of drawers next to her bed. The same powder blue, digital radio alarm clock that had been her trusted friend and never let her down until. . .

It was flashing, blink, blinking away, and the time read 03:42.

Declan was right, which was something that didn't happen very often! Jess groaned. She hated being late and having to rush around. Mornings were for easing you gently into the day, not firing you into it as if you'd just been shot out of a cannon. It was a school day too and running late for school was an unimaginable thing to happen to someone who was always up and ready before everyone else. Jess was the sort of girl who arrived early, finished projects ahead of time and never skipped homework. You know the type.

She sprang to attention, no longer the bleary-eyed zombie, and rushed over to her desk, grappling around in the semi-darkness until she found her watch. Turning on the desk light, she saw it was 7:30 and a lump dropped to the pit of her stomach where it bounced around like a rubber ball, adding to the sick feeling she already had due to morning hunger pangs.

Plenty of people get up after 7:30 and still make it to work and school on time. Not if they live in a village. One where the only way to get to school is by train and the train leaves at 8:00 and you live fifteen minutes' walk away from the station and you can't leave home without showering, washing your hair or eating breakfast!

Jess screamed. Once she'd stopped screaming, her brain switched to attack-mode and she ran towards the bathroom just as Declan swung the door open. He bombed out. His big, burly frame almost knocking her over, but used to his bumbling ways, Jess avoided colliding with him just in time.

"Mum's car. Station. Ten to," he said, or at least that's what it sounded like. He still had his toothbrush in his mouth, so the words came out all spitty, along with white blobs of toothpaste, which Jess had to dodge as she pushed past him.

In her mind, Jess did the calculation. She had twenty minutes to get ready, which meant prioritising. Deciding cleanliness was preferable to breakfast, Jess dived in and out of the shower, then dressed for school, fumbling with the buttons on her shirt. It wasn't until she got to the last one, she realised they were done up wrong, but there was no time to re-do them. Feeling uncomfortable, in tights twisted round the wrong way and wet hair dripping down her back, she grabbed her school bag and ran downstairs. Her mum was shouting at them to hurry and get in the car.

Declan threw an apple in Jess's direction, which she tried to catch but missed, picking it up from the floor and shoving it in her bag anyway, knowing it would develop a horrible bruised bit. She added a banana and a cereal bar and hobbled out of the door after him, shoes half on and half off her feet. Risking catching a cold by going out with wet hair in wintertime and threatening to ruin her school shoes by bending the backs down was against everything Jess stood for and it was making her feel queasy.

She plonked into the car, almost tripping up as she did so, and slammed the door shut just as her mum set off out of the drive, as though they were leaving the starting line of the Grand Prix.

They hadn't gone far when they reached a set of temporary traffic lights that seemed to have magically appeared overnight. For a moment Jess wondered whether they might be stuck on red.

Her mum shouted at them as if they were able to hear her. "Come on, change, will you? Are you even working? They're not working, are they? There's no one coming from the other side, I'm going through if they don't change in a minute. Come on! Change!"

Neither Jess nor Declan spoke, which was unusual for Declan. Jess shrank down in her seat and thought she might die of embarrassment if her mum went through a temporary traffic light on red. She concentrated on re-doing her shirt buttons, taking advantage of the fact the car was stationary. As the lights changed and the car sped through, it swayed, hurling both Jess and Declan to one side and then the other, causing Jess to bump her head on the window.

"Ouch! That hurt," she said, rubbing at what was sure to be a bruise and feeling just like her poor apple.

"Sorry, Jess, you all right? Nearly there."

She didn't want to seem ungrateful—Mum was going out of her way to take them to the station after all—but Jess was relieved their journey was nearly over.

Declan and Jess jumped out of the car the moment it screeched to a halt outside the ticket office.

"Doors!" Mum shouted as they ran off, leaving the doors wide open in their rush to get to the train.

Doing a speedy about-turn, Jess and her brother hurried back, shutting the doors just in time, before their mum sped off again.

"Laters," Declan said to Jess, as he took the stairs two at a time, up to the bridge that led towards the platform at the far side. Even though they went to the same school, they didn't sit together on the train. Declan was far too cool for that, and besides, Jess wouldn't want to anyway. She and her friends had their own usual spot on the platform and she was sure they'd all be waiting there already, wondering where she was. She was just about to set off towards the stairs, when the three of them came running towards her, puffing their way up the hill.

"You're late too?" Jess said, stating the obvious, she knew, but the morning was starting to feel just a little too strange and it was unnerving her.

"What a nightmare, you won't believe what happened this morning," Nadia said, panting as she held onto Jess with one arm, bent over and trying to catch her breath.

"Save it for the train. It's here—look?" Tomma said. "Come on, let's go."

Typical of Tomma, he always took on the role of leader in the group, even though he was actually the youngest of the four of them. Jess didn't mind though and Ash was so easy-going he was almost horizontal. It was Nadia whom it bothered the most. She was just as strong a character as Tomma and didn't like to feel as though she was being told what to do.

Not that she had time to argue. The four of them dashed towards the stairs and Jess tried to take them two at a time like her brother had but failed on account of being much less fit and having shorter legs. Tomma and Ash steamed ahead, as did Nadia.

"Come on, Jess, hurry!" Nadia said, waving her hand as if by pure magic she could lure Jess towards her.

"Down this way," Ash said, directing them towards a hedge where they could get through to the platform.

Although it was a shortcut to the platform, no one ever used it because it went to the farthest end, which few trains were long enough to reach. The children didn't have any choice though and, when they squeezed through, they were within reach, just about, of the very last part of the very last carriage of the train.

The whistle blew.

Chapter 3

The Steam Train

"Get in, quick!" Tomma said, shoving Jess in first, then Nadia, before jumping in behind Ash.

Almost a head and shoulders taller than the rest of them, Tomma could have easily passed for a couple of years older. His dad was the local rugby coach and an ex-professional player and Tomma was built the same way, seeming to have grown almost daily in the last year.

Jess remembered when they'd been the same height, but now she found herself looking up at him and he didn't look out of place at secondary school at all, not like the other timid little Year Sevens with their oversized blazers and rucksacks almost as big as them. Tomma had the confidence of someone who was comfortable in their own skin. Tomma, with the jet-black hair, along with those unusual almond-shaped eyes— something that hadn't gone unnoticed by the other girls in their year. Jess had seen the way some of them looked at him and she knew it shouldn't irritate her, but it did.

The door clicked shut as Tomma pulled it closed before flopping down next to Jess. Everyone was breathing hard, too shocked to speak, at least for the first few minutes anyway.

"Woo-hoo, that was awesome!" Ash said. "Didn't think we were going to make it on here. Did you see what I did taking us down that short cut? Genius I am." He sat back, hands interlocked over his stomach, looking as though he'd just won a Nobel Prize.

"Did you have a power cut last night too?" Jess asked. She lived on the opposite side of the village to Nadia, Ash and Tomma, who all lived within two streets of each other.

"Yeah, my clock was flashing 3:42 when Mum came in and woke me up," Nadia said.

Jess, in her laidback, relaxed position, suddenly sat up straight and stared at Nadia with her eyes wide. "Mine said that too."

"I don't need an alarm clock. Anit is always awake at 6.30, alarm or no alarm," Ash said. He pulled a face, but everyone knew he doted on his baby sister, no matter what she did.

"Didn't make any difference to me either. I had my phone in my room anyway," Tomma said.

"You're allowed your phone in your room? Lucky! The only thing I'm allowed in my room is study books. Might as well be locked in there until I'm eighteen," Ash said.

He mimed a noose being tightened around his neck, making the noise of someone choking. Jess elbowed him in the ribs. Despite his strict family, Ash always managed to make a joke about his situation, somehow accepting of the way things were.

Jess shivered. It was only a power cut, but something didn't feel quite right to her. She was also easily spooked by anything out of the ordinary. Tomma was looking at her as if she was crazy, but he, of all people, knew what she could be like; they'd been the closest out of the four of them. Until recently that was. Jess had noticed things between them had become awkward and could tell Tomma had similar feelings. Although she liked being around him, Jess felt shy in his company, yet whenever he wasn't there, she missed him. She threw him a hurt glare and at least he had the decency to look sorry.

"I've been running around the garden trying to catch Anit's rabbit," Ash said. "Today of all days the stupid thing decided to do a runner. Mum was going hysterical because she said Anit loves that bunny and she'll be devastated if it escapes."

"Look at the state of this," Nadia said, seemingly ignoring Ash as she pulled at her long brown curls. "I almost got blown up by my hairdryer. Then my brush got stuck and I thought I would have to come to school with it still stuck in, but Mum helped pull it out. She had to cut a bit of hair off though. What a nightmare!"

"I spilt cereal all down my uniform and Mum made me change," Tomma said. "I don't know why. I said it didn't matter, but she wasn't having any of it. She always insists we turn up smart wherever we're going."

Power cut or not, they had all had crazy mornings, causing them to be late and almost miss the train. Jess was glad she wasn't the only one feeling a little 'off' that day and she began to relax, laughing along with the others, as they competed for who had had the worst time of it. But as she looked around the carriage, something struck her as strange and a feeling of unease began to creep back over her.

"This train is ancient," she said. "And why are we the only ones on here?"

The first thing Jess thought of was the Hogwarts Express from *Harry Potter* and she blinked as she looked around. They'd bumbled in, without even thinking about it, and were now sat inside an enclosed carriage that had two benches, one opposite the other, the seats of which were covered in a scratchy carpet-like red material that was almost bare from years of being sat on. A musty smell lingered in the air and the carriage was dark and gloomy due to all the dark wood on the walls and doors. Outside of the sliding glass doors of the little compartment, was a narrow corridor that ran along the length of the carriage. There was an identical seating compartment next to theirs but that one was empty.

"You have got to be kidding," Nadia said, noticing her surroundings for the first time too. She didn't seem phased by it though, more irritated than anything else. "Have they brought this train out of the museum or something?"

She pulled her jacket closer around her, turning her nose up at the smell and shifting from side to side as she looked at the thread-bare seating.

"Why is there no one else in here?" Jess repeated, the silence of the carriage unnerving her.

Usually packed at that time of day—the school kids having to share the train with commuters —the friends never got a seat, yet there they were in a carriage all to themselves.

"We are on the right train, aren't we?" Jess stood up and was about to step out of the carriage when Nadia pulled at her coat, forcing her to sit back down with a thump.

"Relax, Jess, it's probably because we're at the back," Nadia said, rubbing Jess's arm in an attempt to soothe her friend, even though it was likely to be futile. "Sometimes they add extra carriages. We've never been this far down ! never know, this could be here every day and we just ⌣ notice it."

"Yeah, but it does look like it's come straight from the transport museum," Ash said. "I know because I went there in the summer. I'm not surprised no one else is on here, it stinks!"

"It doesn't make sense. Something doesn't feel right to me," said Jess, standing up again.

Nadia scowled at Ash. "Nice one, now look what you've done. You're freaking Jess out." She gave him a look that warned him to keep his mouth shut and then turned her attention back to Jess who was nibbling at her thumbnail and looking close to tears. Nadia turned to Tomma for inspiration. If anyone could calm Jess down, it was him.

"Ah, well, who's complaining?" Tomma said. "I'm just going to enjoy having a seat to myself for once." He stretched out his long legs, resting his hands at the back of his head.

Nadia looked to the heavens and shook her head, muttering under her breath about useless people having no idea, before standing up and stepping out of the carriage to look around.

"It does seem slow though," she said, as she peered out of the window. "And it smells like the steam railway I went on at Christmas when I was little, but don't worry, Jess, I'm sure it's all fine. We're moving, aren't we?"

At that moment, the train gave a loud 'toot toot' and the children looked at each other and frowned.

Jess was sure she could hear the 'chugga chugga' sound of an old steam train. She got up, stepping out of the compartment and into the corridor to join Nadia. The train had picked up speed but was only moving at a steady pace, not zooming along as it usually did. Jess tried the door through to the next carriage. It was locked. She tried to see through, but the glass was too dark.

Another loud hoot caused her to jump and she screeched, "Doesn't do that normally," before backing into the compartment and sitting down next to Tomma, almost knocking Nadia over in her haste.

"Stop panicking, it's fine," Nadia said, poking her head into the compartment as she leaned against the sliding doors. "So, it's an old train, who cares? Still works, doesn't it? I think it's cool."

Jess wished she were more like her friend. Nothing seemed to bother Nadia, unlike Jess who found everything difficult and stressful. Nadia would always throw herself into anything headfirst, without stopping to think about the consequences. Jess had to analyse everything to the Nth degree before she would even attempt it. She wondered if being so different was what made them such good friends.

Ash got up and went into the corridor, pulling down the top part of the door to stick his head out of the window.

"Ash, don't," Jess leapt up and tugged on his coat to pull him back in. Her heart was almost in her mouth. "What if we go through a tunnel and your head gets chopped off?"

She'd heard about that happening before. It was the sort of big-brotherly wisdom that Declan was so fond of telling her, or showing her on YouTube and giving her nightmares forevermore.

"I'm just having a look, that's all. It's cool, you should see."

Jess backed away and Ash laughed, though not cruelly.

"You won't believe it unless you see," he said, shouting above the noise of the engine. "It's a steam train, all of it."

Tomma jumped up, pushing Jess out of the way. He came to join Nadia and Ash and the three of them took turns to put their heads out of the window, making sounds of 'ooh' and 'ahh,' seeming not to care that it was freaking Jess out.

She sat back down on one of the benches and stared around at the empty carriage, thinking once again about the ghosts of the past that Mrs Kennedy had talked about in their history lesson. Who had travelled in this train and what were their stories? Had they put their luggage on the wire racks above the seats and sat looking out of the window as the world passed by? Were they going to Leeds? Or further afield to York? Scarborough? Why today of all days, when everything seemed to have gone wrong so far, did they end up sitting alone in this strange train? There were so many questions racing around in her mind that Jess didn't even notice the others come back in.

It felt as though the train was alive, pulsing along the tracks, the movement providing a rhythmic beat that was both hypnotic and soothing. Nadia got out her phone and after staring at it for a few seconds, she shook it before holding it in the air and sighing.

"I haven't got a signal, have you?"

The others checked theirs and they all showed 'no service.'

Nadia threw her phone back into her bag and got out her book instead. Jess ate her snacks, absentmindedly staring out of the window again, back into thoughts of the past, only faintly registering the boys chuckling away at her side. But then the train hooted again, so loud it caused Jess to jump. The others laughed.

"Urgh, it stinks! Shut the window, someone," Nadia said, holding her nose.

Tomma got up and Jess tried not to cringe when he looked out of the window again.

"It's the smoke from the engine," he said, pulling the window up to shut it and coming back to sit down. "I can't believe it's a proper old steam train. Wait 'til we tell the others at school."

"If we ever get to school," Jess said. "What time is it anyway? This thing seems to have stopped." She shook her wrist and tapped at her watch. The others checked theirs and they all had no service.

No phone signal, all their watches had stopped and they had no idea what the time was. Even so, Jess could tell that at the speed the train was travelling there was no way they would get to school on time.

Chapter 4

Where's Our School?

When the train arrived at Hickley, the big old clock face that hung suspended from the painted-metal internal framework of the Victorian station was just beginning to chime. It was a quarter to nine, which meant the usual twenty-minute journey had taken forty-five and the children had just five minutes to get to school before registration.

"Oh great," Nadia said, as she looked up at the clock. "What's going on today? We seem to be late for everything."

She adjusted the bag strap on her shoulder and was just about to look around when Tomma pushed through to take his position at the front of the pack.

"We're going to have to leg it up the road," Tomma said. "Come on."

The slow, bumpy train journey, coupled with the stress of worrying about what was going on, had left Jess feeling a little sick. The thought of having to run up the hill to school made her feel worse, but she knew she had no choice so she set off after the others. They were in such a hurry that they barely noticed just how different their surroundings were, such as the Shire horse and carriage waiting outside the station, even as they stepped over a large pile of horse dung that made their nostrils curl.

They didn't stop to wonder about how old-fashioned the cars were and why the roads were cobbled instead of tarmacked smooth; why women were dressed in long skirts, with matching jackets and hats, whilst men whizzed by in top hats and long-tailed jackets. None of that registered at that moment, as all their focus was on getting to school. The world around them was nothing but a blur.

On reaching the main playground of Hickley School, they all stopped and doubled over, breathing hard. The feeling of unease Jess had on the train grew stronger, as she looked around, taking it all in for the first time. The main building of the school looked familiar, but somehow it seemed newer; the black, soot-stained Yorkshire stone had been cleaned overnight and was now the colour of golden sand. Directly in front of them should have been the dining hall, but it was missing and to the right, there was no sports hall either. Whole buildings had somehow disappeared overnight.

As they stood in bewilderment, wondering just what to make of it all, a boy jogged over to them. He looked about their age, but Jess didn't recognise him. His uniform, though the familiar dark brown with brown and yellow striped tie, was unusual in that he had teamed it with a full, buttoned-up, waistcoat, and trousers that ended just below the knee.

"What you doing in our yard?" He was looking at Nadia and Jess. "If Crawford catches ya, you'll cop it."

The girls looked at him then at each other. Neither had noticed they were the only girls in the playground, which was normally full of pupils from all years. No one around looked familiar and it was as if all the pupils had been replaced with a new set.

"This is a bit weird," Nadia said, whispering in Jess's ear. "Is there something going on today we don't know about?"

"I don't know," said Jess. "But the school looks different. How can buildings be missing? It's creeping me out. Shall we go see if we can find the other girls?"

Jess was desperate to find something, or someone, familiar, otherwise, she didn't know what to think.

"Yeah, good idea, come on. We'll see you at break time," Nadia said to Tomma and Ash, as she linked arms with Jess and they set off across the yard towards the main doors.

They'd only got halfway across when a loud bell sounded. It wasn't the usual steady, beating pulse of the school bell. Someone was standing at the door with an actual bell in his hand, shaking it up and down in a slow, rhythmic motion.

Jess jumped and clutched Nadia tighter as they stopped, wondering what they should do next. They watched as the boys in the yard started to form neat lines. The bell seeming to be the only prompt they needed to make them comply.

"What are they doing?" Jess asked in a quivery voice.

"What are they wearing?" Nadia said, looking them up and down with distaste.

It was typical of Nadia to notice that, Jess thought, but she had a point. Everyone was dressed the same way as the boy they'd spoken to. Most were wearing flat caps and some had on duffle coats.

"Is it a dress-up day?" Nadia said.

Too absorbed in what was going on around them, they

didn't notice the man with the bell striding towards them at a determined pace, his mouth set in a tight line.

"What are you doing here? Get around to the girls' yard at once!" he said, snapping his fingers and thrusting his arm in the direction of the door he'd just come from.

Jess's first thought was how freakishly long his finger seemed as it pointed the way. She looked at Nadia, whose expression was blank. The man, whom they presumed was a teacher, let out an exasperated sigh that made the large moustache on his upper lip quiver.

"Well go on then! What are you waiting for?" He stepped aside, holding out his arm in an open gesture towards the door.

Although Jess opened her mouth to speak, no words would come out. She had no idea what the man was talking about and it must have shown in both her and Nadia's expressions. Losing his patience, he grabbed Nadia by the arm, marching her towards the door.

"What are you doing?" she yelled, trying to free her arm, determination set in her face. Being an only child, Nadia was used to getting her own way and being treated like a princess.

Even so, Jess was shocked at how rough the teacher was being. No teacher she knew would treat pupils this way—princess or not. The man, who was not in the slightest bit phased, became more exasperated than ever.

"You clearly have no regard for my authority and I haven't got the time to deal with you right now, so you will go through to the girls' yard and I will see to it that Miss Yardley deals with you in the correct manner."

He stared at them with a look that could turn someone

to stone and in a desperate plea for help, Jess turned to look at Tomma and Ash, who both shrugged, equally as dumbfounded as they were. Angry at their response, she huffed, before turning and hurrying to catch up to Nadia.

Shuffling along behind her, she glanced anxiously around. Everyone in the playground was staring at them with open mouths. Jess inwardly cringed, knowing on the outside, she would be beetroot red from head to toe.

When the teacher eventually let go of Nadia's arm, she brushed at her jacket to straighten it out, glaring at him all the while. Without speaking, he merely pointed towards the end of the corridor and nodded his head in the same direction.

"Come on," Jess said, pulling Nadia along before she could say anything else and get into more trouble.

They walked down the corridor, where at the end on the left were doors leading to another yard. As Nadia pushed open the heavy glass doors, Jess stood close behind her, looking tentatively over her friend's shoulder.

This yard was full of girls, dressed in long, dark-brown pinafores, heavily pleated down the front and cinched in at the waist with matching belts. They had on white, scalloped-necked, long-sleeved blouses, but no tie. Some wore overcoats, others had shawls. There was a female teacher, standing with a bell in her hand, inspecting the lines. She had on a floor-length, heavy-duty, black skirt and white blouse and some kind of sleeved cape that made her look more like a witch than a teacher. Her hair was tied neatly in a low bun, which made her features even sterner.

"You're late! Get in line now," she said, glaring at Jess and Nadia, which nearly made Jess faint with fear. Even Nadia was quick to move and they scrambled to the back of the first line they came to.

"Hi. . . sorry, is this the Year Seven line?" Jess whispered to the girl at the end, as she stood in line behind her.

The girl put her head down and turned it slightly so she could whisper back, "What are you on about? This is the First Form."

Not knowing what to make of that reply, Jess shrugged and gave Nadia a blank look. Then, realising the line was beginning to move, she stared at the floor and followed the other girls as they filed into the school building. The sick feeling in Jess's stomach began to worsen. All she wanted to do was get to her form room and find out from her teacher what was going on.

"What is the meaning of this. . . this attire?" the bell-ringing teacher said, blocking Jess and Nadia's path, and looking down at them with the face of someone who had just been sucking on a lemon.

Jess jumped, as she came to a sudden halt, almost causing Nadia to walk straight into her. She put her head down, not daring to look the teacher directly in the eye, and watched the lower halves of the other girls get further and further away from them.

"What do you mean, Miss? This is what we always wear," Nadia said.

"Don't answer back, girl."

"But you asked us a question."

"I said, don't answer back. What is the matter with you?"

"But you—" Nadia began.

"Nadia!" Jess nudged her in the back.

Didn't she know when to be quiet?

"Since when do girls wear ties?" she said, flicking Nadia's tie in the air with her fingertip. "And what is the meaning of these short skirts? It's quite disgraceful showing so much flesh. Get to Matron's office at once and see to it she finds you some of the correct uniforms from the spares box. I don't want to see you looking like this again, do you understand?"

The girls both nodded.

"I said, do you understand?" Her raised voice made Jess straighten up alongside Nadia. She felt as if they were army recruits.

"Yes, Miss," both girls chorused.

"What did she mean by that?" Jess said once they were out of earshot and on their way to Matron's office. "I don't remember getting a letter that said we had changed uniforms. Mum is gonna be so cross."

Nadia sighed, before stopping to turn to Jess. "I'm not going to lie, this is all feeling a bit weird. Don't freak out but there is something strange going on today. Look at the school. It's all clean and new for a start and where's the sports block and dining hall?" Nadia's eyes danced with excitement. "What if we've travelled back in time?"

Jess whacked her on the arm. "Do not even say that. You read too many fantasy books you do."

"But think about it, how else do you explain all this?" Nadia was getting into her idea. "Buildings are missing and the school looks new. Maybe this is what it looked like when it was first opened?"

"Shut up Nadia, you're freaking me out. Let's just get to Matron's office and sort out the uniform so we don't get in trouble with that teacher again." Jess didn't want to listen to any theory about time travel. All she wanted to do was find some semblance of normality and cling on to that, hoping everything else would start to make sense eventually.

"That is, if Matron's office is there..."

Jess groaned. There was a possibility this was all a bad dream and she would wake up soon, finding everything as it should be, and there hadn't been a power cut after all. She concentrated on that, ignoring Nadia's comment, as she marched on ahead.

Chapter 5

War? What War?

To Jess's relief, they found the office in the place where they expected it to be—right at the far end of the school in the downstairs of the Sixth Form annexe. However, Matron looked more like Florence Nightingale than Mrs Mortimer, whom they were used to. This particular school nurse was wearing a floor-length, full-sleeved uniform complete with a short cape that fitted around her shoulders. She even had on a funny little hairpiece that hung down her back a bit like a veil.

Jess was thankful that the kindly-looking nurse didn't shout at them or question why they were dressed so differently. On being asked, she merely handed them each a set of clothes in what she thought were the right size and told them where they could change. Both girls were in too much shock to ask her what was happening to their school.

"This day just gets weirder," Nadia said in a low voice as she looked at the clothes.

They were in a room that had a small, metal-framed camp bed in the corner. There was a sink to the right of an open fireplace and a desk under the window, the glass of which was obscured so no one could see in.

The material of the pinafores was so stiff and itchy. Once they'd both put theirs on and fastened the belts, the bottom half of the dresses stuck straight out at each side. Nadia desperately tried to smooth hers down but to no avail. The blouses were just as bad, the material stiff, with no give to them whatsoever. Beginning to see the funny side, Nadia looked at Jess and laughed.

"You don't look so great yourself," Jess said. "I hope they haven't changed the uniform permanently. I am not wearing this thing every day." She grabbed the sides of her skirt, pulling at the scratchy material and frowning in disgust. She put her own clothes into her bag.

"Come on, let's get to class." Nadia put an arm around her shoulder and gave it a gentle squeeze. The gesture was enough to make Jess cry, but she managed to hold in the tears by taking a few deep, calming breaths to still her wobbly chin.

They left Matron's office and walked back to where they'd come from. There was no one around; everyone else having gone to their form rooms. Jess was hoping they wouldn't bump into anyone and could make it to their own form room unseen, but unfortunately, the female teacher who had sent them to Matron happened to be walking along the corridor at the same time. Jess felt herself shrink as she moved closer to Nadia's side.

"Ah, there you are. That's better," the teacher said, looking them up and down. "Get to your form room now. Quick, hurry along, no talking."

"I guess we just go to our usual room and hope for the best," Nadia said, in a low voice.

"I said, no talking!"

The girls stifled giggles as they did their best to shuffle along in the full-length dresses. Their usual registration room was off the main hall, which meant they had to retrace their steps back along the corridor, but this time, instead of going left into the girls' yard, they turned right, going through the doors into the main hall, then turning left towards one of the classrooms that led off it.

As soon as they pushed open the door and stepped tentatively into the classroom, all hopes of a normal day faded. The room looked like someone had transformed it overnight by knocking down a wall to double its size. Their usual desks were gone, replaced with some old-fashioned wooden ones with lids you could lift to put your things inside. These weren't the graffiti-marked, battered old desks Jess was used to seeing at her school. The desks in front of Jess and Nadia looked new and, in a way, they were kind of beautiful with wood so smooth and flat it made Jess want to reach out and stroke her hand along the surface.

Sitting at a larger desk at the front of the classroom was not Mr Ward, the girls' usual form teacher. He, along with the desks, had also been replaced. In his place sat a lady dressed in a long, black cloak with her hair in a tight grey bun and round glasses perched on the very end of her nose. She looked over the glasses at Jess and Nadia as they stood unsure what to do.

"Ah, Chadwick and Kaminski there you are. Good of you to join us."

Jess thought she detected a hint of sarcasm in her tone, rather than one of actual pleasure at their arrival. She braced herself for another shouting at but the teacher turned back to her desk and put two ticks on the page in front of her.

There were only two empty desks left in the classroom, one at the front and the other right at the back. Jess bolted towards the furthest one, throwing an apologetic look at Nadia. Scanning the room, she didn't see one single person she recognised, and the resulting fear and panic made her feel sick again. She was glad to be able to sit at the back of the classroom and hide.

"We will begin morning lessons with arithmetic, but first, it is time for assembly, girls. Please line up and make your way into the hall in an orderly fashion. Do you all have your hymn books?"

Jess rummaged around in her bag and found her copy. She clutched it close to her chest as though it was the most precious thing in the world. It felt comforting to have something familiar, even if it was only a little blue book with hymns in. It was also a relief to see everyone else had the same book.

She was just about to stand when the girl to her right leaned over and put a hand on her arm. It was the same girl from the back of the line in the yard.

"You new?" she asked.

Jess stared at the girl. Her thoughts were too incoherent to process. Not only was she confused about the situation: the change in teacher, the different layout of the classroom, the pupils, the uniforms, but in addition, she couldn't help but gawp at the girl's hair. It was the most beautiful shade of auburn Jess had ever seen, like a canopy of autumn leaves lit up by the setting sun.

"I'm Martha Stenchion," the girl said, in barely a whisper and seemingly oblivious to Jess's dumbstruck state. Martha's head darted to the side to check the teacher wasn't looking. "We get people like you here all the time now. Since the bombs started, there've been more. Orphans, are you? Who've you lost? My brother is away. Haven't heard anything for a while. Dad came home because of a shrapnel wound. He's in hospital still, but at least he's back now, thank the Lord."

Martha looked so sad and lost. Jess found herself wanting to reach out to Martha, even though she had no idea what Martha was talking about, but she didn't have time. The other girls were standing up and beginning to form a line in front of the door.

Jess followed them, behind Martha, as the line headed out of the classroom and down towards the front of the hall. Martha's words stuck with her, riding around her head with everything else, but she told herself to stop being such a worrier and that everything was going to be fine. Nadia, who was nearer the front of the line and now a few rows ahead of her, turned around. Jess caught her eye.

Nadia mouthed, "You okay?"

Jess nodded back, forcing a smile, before concentrating on finding the right hymn number.

Assembly began in the usual way, with a hymn, followed by a prayer. Normally the Headteacher led the assembly, but in his place stood a bald man with small round glasses. He wore a black suit, the jacket of which reached down to the back of his knees. Under the jacket was a pinstripe waistcoat, with a chain hanging down between the two pockets. Standing before them in silence, he pulled at the chain and brought out the pocket watch at the end of it. After checking the time, he tucked the watch away again. He began to speak.

First, there were some general announcements about a debating club meeting and a chess tournament. All seemed normal and non-eventful until the man began to talk about the war. At this, Jess straightened up, feeling all her senses go on full alert, her skin go cold and goosebumps begin to form on her arms and the back of her neck. The man read out the names of two former pupils of the school who had died, along with a short eulogy, then he said how proud he was to have known them.

"Let's all pray for their families in their hour of need,"

The room fell silent as everyone bowed their heads.

With her heart beating out of her chest, Jess wished she had Nadia by her side. Her head was spinning with all the talk of war and death and bombs; she didn't know what to think. The man began to speak again and everyone raised their heads to look back up at him.

"The war is close to an end," he said. "We hope to hear of the Allies signing a peace treaty with Germany very soon."

Jess looked at Nadia, who had turned around to seek her out. Nadia's face was white, her eyes wide and, as Jess looked towards the boys, searching for Tomma and Ash, she could see they had turned a funny shade of pale too. Then her vision began to blur and she could feel her body start to sway. Before Jess had time to do anything about it, the world went black.

Chapter 6

All Is Not As It Seems

Jess came around to see Matron hovering over her, wafting something under her nose. The smell was sharp and pungent like vinegar. It made Jess cough and her eyes water.

"There you go, that should do it. Don't sit up too quickly," Matron said. "You just fainted."

After what they'd heard in assembly, it was no surprise that Jess had fainted. Jess was now positive something strange had happened that morning and there was no getting away from that fact. It was becoming clear whatever had happened had affected them in a big way, like in a going-back-in-time way. Nadia might have been joking when she'd said it, but now Jess was beginning to wonder whether she might have been right.

Jess's head spun, not just from fainting, but with the possibility of it all. It's not every day you travel back in time, is it? And to a war! What war? The man, whoever he was, hadn't said. Jess wondered if he was the Headteacher at Hickley School. The Head always conducted assembly. As for going back in time, that wasn't possible surely? Jess still clung to the hope it was all a strange dream, but that hope was fading by the minute.

Feeling uncomfortable on the cold, hard, wooden floor, she shifted and rolled onto her side, coming up to a sitting position. She tried to focus so she wouldn't black out again. There was no one left in the hall apart from Nadia, Matron and Martha. Martha was looking down at Jess with concern. Her brightly coloured hair falling down the front of her chest, lighting up her pale face.

"Don't just stand there girls! Help me get your friend up," Matron said, staring hard at Nadia, who looked like she was in a world of her own, probably a world that involved twenty-first-century technology. Nadia came to her senses and took Jess's hands to help her stand.

"I think you'll be just fine. I have to get back to my office now. Would you girls be so kind as to take your friend to her classroom?" Matron asked.

Martha and Nadia nodded enthusiastically, both immediately moving to each side of Jess, supporting her arms.

"You okay?" Nadia said.

"Not really, you?"

Nadia shook her head, looking grave. "I almost fainted too when I heard what he said, and it looked like Tomma and Ash were going to go the same way. What are we going to do?"

It wasn't often Nadia asked that sort of question to Jess. It was usually the other way around and Nadia was the one who came up with a solution.

"I don't know. My head hurts just thinking about it."

Jess began to sway a little, but Nadia and Martha kept a firm grip on her arms. They led her over to the side of the hall, where there was a small wooden bench. The three of them sat down, elbows on knees, resting their chins upon their hands.

"Probably from when you bumped it on the floor," Nadia said, turning her face towards Jess.

"Not in the mood for jokes, Nad."

"Sorry, can't help myself." Nadia's eyebrows shot up as she cocked her head to one side and smiled with an air of nonchalance.

Jess let out a long sigh before rubbing at her temples where she could feel a headache beginning to form. She turned her attention towards Martha on her other side. Not knowing whether they should be back in their form rooms or somewhere else, Jess was grateful to have Martha with them.

"Don't worry, it's not that bad here," Martha said. "Some of them don't want the likes of you here. It reminds them of what they've lost themselves or might lose. Most of them are all right though."

"Is that why no one took any notice of Jess when she fainted?" Nadia said, her expression more serious now. "You wouldn't believe it! They acted like you weren't even there. No one seemed to care."

"Folks are always fainting round here. Some have to walk miles to school every day and with food so scarce, they don't always have 'owt to eat. We're all starving."

That brought things into perspective. These people were in the middle of a war and as well as losing their loved ones, they had no food. It made Jess feel desperate on their part.

"Come on, do you think you can walk now?" Martha said. "We have to get to class. Miss Jennings will be wondering where we are and she isn't shy to use the cane."

Jess shuddered, standing up and taking a deep breath. This was the most surreal of situations and they were stuck at school whether they liked it or not. She knew she was going to have to tough it out for the time being, until they knew more about what had happened to them. Martha's situation was very sobering. There were obvious difficulties going on for everyone around them, yet Martha seemed so strong and accepting. Jess and her friends had none of these troubles to deal with. Their lives were easy in comparison—disregarding their current situation that is.

As the girls trudged slowly towards the classroom in silence, they passed Tomma and Ash, who were at the back of a queue of boys filing out of the door. Tomma looked at Jess in concern. She nodded to let him know she was okay.

"Where are you going?" she mouthed.

Tomma shrugged before pointing to the door.

"Outside," he said but it was clear he had no idea why.

Jess wished they were all together in class as they usually were but was reassured when Tomma raised a smile back at her. He was comfortable with the situation, whatever it happened to be and just knowing he was around made Jess feel better somehow.

Chapter 7

Back To The Old School

Martha led them back to the classroom they had been in for registration earlier. Usually, the students collected their bags after assembly and went off to lessons. Jess knew that probably wasn't going to happen and she was right. The other girls were all sitting at their desks in silence, watching as Miss Jennings wrote an equation on the blackboard. She stopped and straightened up when they walked in.

"Sorry we're late, Miss. Jess fainted," Martha said.

"Yes, yes, I heard. Come along and sit down. I won't have you disrupting my lesson. Miss Kaminski, perhaps you can come and show the rest of the girls how we solve this equation?"

Jess almost fainted again as Nadia looked at her with her eyes wide. Confident in most ways, the one thing Nadia couldn't bear was standing up and speaking in front of other people. An embarrassing show-and-tell in Year Five had left its mark and was something she was unable to shake off, even two years on.

Poor Nadia, Jess thought, but all she could do was offer a nod of encouragement, as she left her friend standing before the class. Nadia's usual glowing skin looked pale and grey as all the blood had drained from it. Everyone was staring at Nadia, and Jess could see her hands shaking, as she took the chalk from the teacher.

Even though Nadia wasn't confident being singled out in such a way, especially in front of people she didn't know, she was brilliant at maths and Jess knew she would have no problem doing the calculation. Jess held her breath as Nadia turned slowly towards the blackboard. Hesitating for only a moment, she lifted the stick of chalk and began to write.

Jess was relieved, but she could see Nadia was finding it difficult to write on the board with the chalk. It scratched across the dusty black surface, making an occasional screeching noise, that set your nerves on edge like the sound foxes make when they come out at night. Whiteboards were so much easier, but Nadia didn't have that choice and as she continued to scratch away at the blackboard, marking out each part of the equation, the piece of chalk snapped in half. Some of the girls began to snigger, but one glare from Miss Jennings soon silenced them. If Nadia had been bothered by the sniggering, she didn't let on. When she finished, she stood back and looked at the teacher.

"Very good," Miss Jennings said, and began to explain to the rest of the class what Nadia had done.

Jess could tell from the wide grin across Nadia's face that she was both pleased and relieved. So relieved, in fact, that she continued to stand there grinning.

"Don't just stand there!" Miss Jennings snapped. "Wipe the board and take a seat."

Nadia looked helplessly at Miss Jennings before following her gaze to a wooden-handled block. She picked it up and began to scrub at the board. Unfortunately, it not only cleared away the numbers, but it also smeared the chalk all around, covering her in a cloud of chalk dust, which made Nadia sneeze. Again, more sniggers. Jess could feel Nadia's relief as she scuttled back to her seat.

"Take out your books and complete the rest of these," Miss Jennings said, writing on the board again.

Copying Martha, Jess opened her desk and found that inside was a notebook with her name on it. Her thoughts immediately turned to how strange it was that she and Nadia were known to the teachers and even listed on the register. It seemed they were a part of this school no matter what time zone they found themselves in.

She took out the notebook and leant down to reach into her bag, fishing out her pencil case. She put it inside the desk and took out a pen.

"What's that?" Martha said.

"This pen?" Jess whispered back. "You know, what you write with?" She moved her wrist, pretending to write in the air.

"You have to use these otherwise you'll get told off," Martha said. She pointed to a pot of ink hidden in a hole at the edge of the desk.

Jess had wondered what those holes were for when she'd seen desks like these before. In it was a wooden stick and when she picked it up, she saw it was like a fountain pen. She put her own pen away and turned her attention to the task ahead, trying to play it down, but at the same time thinking it was quite exciting to be doing something so different. That novelty soon wore off though.

At first it was fun to dip the nib in and out of the ink but after a while, it became completely frustrating. Each time Jess used it, the ink would go from blotchy to faint, by which time the nib was scratching across the page making it almost impossible to write anything. Her work didn't look neat at all and she worried about being told off. She also kept accidentally catching the side of her hand on the paper, covering it in ink and smudging the writing.

All she could think about was break time and getting out of there, as well as the urge to hurl the pen across the room or stamp on it until it was nothing more than a broken twig.

Break time never came though and the maths lesson dragged on. Afterwards they moved on to English. The girls were reading Shakespeare's *Twelfth Night*, which was strange because Jess and Nadia were reading that in their normal English lessons. They were even on the same page.

Jess loved English so was happy to read along and listen to the discussion. The other girls had the same ideas they'd been discussing and she forgot about being stuck in another time zone. They were simply a group of girls talking about a play by a famous author.

By now, Jess's stomach was rumbling uncontrollably, as if it had a mind of its own. It was so loud it caused her to clutch it in embarrassment and it was hard to imagine how some of the others must have felt having not had any breakfast that morning. At least she'd had a few snacks, even if it was on the run. Jess realised she had no lunch with her and wondered what she would do about that, especially if food was as scarce as Martha had suggested.

As Jess looked around the room, she was reminded of what Mrs Kennedy had said in their history lesson about how children before them had sat in the same classroom. It struck her that she was currently sat among some of those very children, and their lessons, although different in some ways, were not so unfamiliar.

The environment in which they were learning was much stricter though. The children seemed genuinely wary of the teacher as if they were scared of what she might do. Martha had mentioned how Miss Jennings would use the cane on them, something that they luckily didn't have to endure in their own lives.

Miss Jennings set the girls to work writing about how love and romance are depicted in the play. Although Jess had ideas, she found it hard to write them down because of the pen and ink situation. Normally a fast writer, so as not to forget what was in her head, she found working with the quill torture. It was a long morning and by the time the bell rang, Jess was uncomfortable and stiff all over.

"See you later. I've got to go and get my little sister," Martha said, jumping up and shrugging on her duffle coat.

Jess tried not to look at the worn patches and holes at the elbows and pockets and thankfully, Martha didn't seem to notice. She was in too much of a hurry to get away. Jess stayed in her seat watching the others file out of the room until there was only her and Nadia left. She got up and went over to Nadia.

"That was such a long morning, my brain hurts," Jess said, flopping over Nadia's desk.

"I know! What happened to break time? I'm starving. We were supposed to find Tomma and Ash too. I wonder how they got on." Nadia let out a low, long sigh as she began to put her things away. She waved the notebook at Jess. "What's this all about? A book with our name on it. We don't even come to this school!" She threw the book in the desk and stood up to put her jacket on.

"We do technically, even if it's not in this time," Jess said.

"Well you know what I mean. How weird does that sound though? We need to find out what's happening here," Nadia said. "I don't like the way she picked on me as well. It was so unfair."

Jess linked arms with her and pulled her close. "I know, but you did amazing. You should be proud. Let's go see if we can find the others now. Do you think we'll be allowed in the boys' yard?"

"Probably not but unless that teacher is there, I'm going in anyway. You coming?"

Chapter 8

Digging For Victory

Nadia swung her bag over her shoulder as Jess followed her out of the classroom towards the yard they had arrived in that morning.

They peered through the door. "It's empty," Nadia said, looking puzzled. There wasn't a soul out there, as if no one attended the school and they'd imagined all those strangely dressed boys kicking footballs and running around there earlier in the day. They were about to turn around and go back in again when Tomma and Ash appeared behind them.

"We were just looking for you," Ash said. "What a freakish morning, eh?"

"Are you both okay?" Tomma said. He was looking particularly at Jess. "This is all seriously weird. It's like we've come back to another time zone and I can't understand it at all. How could this even happen?"

"I wouldn't even know where to begin explaining this," Nadia said. "I was only half-joking when I said it to Jess earlier. I thought we would get to class and it would all be a big mistake, but when we got there, we didn't know anyone and it was a different teacher. It's completely blown my mind."

"I know what you mean. You should have seen what we had to do all morning. Come on, you've got to see this," Tomma said. "You won't believe it."

Tomma led them out of the yard and away from the school. Separated from the main building was an area where all the sports activities usually took place. Normally, there were tennis courts at the far end and a hockey pitch in the central area, which in summer served as an athletics arena, but in their place was something completely different.

Jess and Nadia both stood with open mouths as they looked around the vast space. It was completely dug over—not in the slightest sports-related, but split into sections, each cordoned off with small wire fences or netting. Jess knew straight away it was an allotment, as she'd been many times to visit her grandad's plot. She shook her head in disbelief as she looked around.

Being November, there wasn't much to see, mostly patches of dirt. Jess guessed that either nothing was growing at that time of year or whatever was growing there was hiding underground, cosy and warm in the soil. There were tools scattered around, wheelbarrows and trugs, spades, forks and even a shed.

"Is this where you've been all morning?" Jess asked, incredulous at the idea the boys had been outside whilst they'd been in a never-ending lesson of maths and English.

"Yep. We walked back into our form room and Crawford— that's the teacher you met this morning—said we had to go straight outside. We had to do our bit for the war effort. He kept going on about digging for victory," Tomma said. "After that assembly, the alarm bells were already ringing, but this just made it worse."

"We didn't know what he was talking about, so we had no choice but to follow the others and they led us up here," Ash said. "Crawford told us to roll up our sleeves and start digging up potatoes over there." He pointed to an area on the near right. Ash was chuckling. "We didn't have a clue, but you know, we knew potatoes grew underground, we're not that stupid, so we just started digging with these long forks he gave us."

"Yeah and when idiot here found one, he only went and shouted it out to everyone, like he'd struck gold or something. Crawford was well impressed with that," Tomma said, shaking his head at Ash and giving him a shove.

"I think the other lads thought we were a bit crazy," Ash said. "But it was fine in the end. Until we started getting hungry and realised we weren't having a break time."

"And did you know everyone goes home at lunch? There's no canteen here," Tomma said.

That shouldn't have come as any surprise. The building housing the dining hall didn't even exist, so it was no shock to find the school didn't provide lunches.

"Oh, I'm starving," Jess said, feeling instantly disappointed. "I didn't have time to make anything this morning."

"Have you got anything?" Nadia said to the boys.

They both nodded.

"Then you can share all of ours Jess," she said. "I'm sure we can sort you something out between us."

There was no discussion. What Nadia said brokered no argument. The boys didn't look too happy about the thought of sharing their food. They were starving too, but they weren't mean enough to not share anything with Jess.

*

"So, what do we do now? I don't want to be stuck here for the rest of my life. I doubt they're going to have hairdryers and decent make-up in this age," Nadia complained.

"Well, we have to find out what's going on," Jess said. "And how to get out of here!"

"You know anything about time travel, then?" Tomma asked. "It was that train wasn't it? And probably the power cut making us late so we had no choice but to get on that carriage."

Jess looked at Nadia, remembering their conversation from earlier. She'd been in denial about it all morning, but really, she knew deep down, it wasn't a dream. This was real.

"Crawford kept talking about the King and how he would be proud of the Hickley Boys for doing their bit towards the war effort," Tomma said, his face set in a serious expression.

"The King?" Jess said. "What year does that make it then?"

"Well, we're in a war and we know it's before Queen Elizabeth's time," Tomma said.

"Was Elizabeth queen in the Second World War?" asked Jess.

"No, I don't think so. She was quite young then, wasn't she?" Tomma said.

"So, how are we going to find out what war we've landed in the middle of?" Nadia said.

"Don't you think it's weird the teachers know our names?"

said Ash. He seemed to have drifted off into his own world, looking out over the allotment.

"That's what me and Jess were saying!" said Nadia. "We even had notebooks with our names on them. But we do come to this school. Maybe we're on the register no matter what time zone we're in?"

They all looked at each other.

"Let's go to the office and see if we can find anything with the date on," Tomma said. Ash slapped him on the back in approval.

"Shouldn't we go to the train station and see if we can get home?" Jess said, feeling suddenly like she was going to cry. By now, she wasn't interested what year it was anymore. She was more concerned about how and if they were ever going to get home. And it wasn't as though she cared about hairdryers and make-up, more about being stuck in another time and never seeing her family again.

"We can do that later, Jess, aren't you even a little bit interested? I mean, come on, how often do you get to go back in time?" Nadia said, her eyes were shining.

Jess had no choice but to follow them, they were so much more curious and adventurous than she was and there was no chance she was going to let them leave her on her own.

Chapter 9

Making A Discovery

The office was deserted. It seemed everyone, including the staff, left for the lunch break and it gave the whole place an eerie feeling.

"Wow, it's like stepping into a museum," Nadia said, walking around, brushing her hands lightly over everything she passed.

The school office, normally kitted out with computers, printers and filing cabinets, was instead adorned with a beautiful dark wooden desk, topped with green leather. In the centre sat a typewriter, something Jess had only ever seen in a picture. Framed posters covered the walls. They had slogans written on them like 'Your Country Needs You' and 'He did his duty, will you do yours?' and there was a man with a thick moustache pointing his finger out towards whoever was looking at it. The room smelled of stale cigarette smoke.

"It's so creepy, isn't it?" Jess said, moving closer to Nadia. "I feel like we're snooping in on something we're not supposed to."

"Well, we are technically," Nadia said. "I doubt pupils

are allowed in here unless invited. It looks all formal and business-like. You'd think they were running the war from in here, not a school."

"Look, I've found something," Tomma said. He pointed to a document on the desk. The date read November the eighth.

"We already know that's today's date," Ash said, rolling his eyes. "We need to know the year."

"There are some notices on the board here," Jess said, moving over to the other side of the room.

On the wall opposite the desk was a large notice board, wooden-framed and made of cork. There was a notice on it that read 'News from Hickley Old Boys' and it had a list of names, each one with a sentence or two about what had happened to them. Some had been shot, another had suffered gas-shell poisoning and there were various injuries mentioned, sustained whilst in 'the trenches.' Jess peered closely at the dates.

"1915, 1916, 1917, 1918. It's the First World War," Jess said.

"So, today is November eighth at some point during the First World War, probably 1918 by the looks of this," Nadia said.

"For some reason, we were meant to get on that train late this morning, so we could come back to this moment in time, but why?" Tomma said. He looked thoughtful, as he bit on his bottom lip, staring at nothing in particular.

For Tomma, having an answer to a question was always the most important thing. Having been one of those toddlers who'd constantly asked, "Why?" he'd taken that curiosity and need-to-know into his childhood and beyond.

Jess shivered. "I don't like the sound of that. What if we

can't get back until we've done whatever it is, we're supposed to do?"

The others looked at her, blank expressions on each of their faces. They didn't know the answer to that either.

*

Needing to get outside, they all went back to the yard to have their lunch. Even though it was cold outside with the sharp November air piercing through the low winter sunshine, it was easier to breathe.

The feeling of being trapped was so strong when they were in the school, especially after having just found out they'd gone back in time, to the end of a war that had had an obvious and profound effect on the local people. Not only were people struggling to find enough to eat, they had also lost friends, family and loved ones for a cause none of them likely really cared for or understood. It was difficult to get your head around it, but once she'd eaten and taken in some fresh air, Jess felt a little better. She even felt brave enough to take a walk around the deserted building with Nadia.

It's strange to encounter something so familiar yet completely different at the same time. The school was beautiful. You could almost see your face in the polished wood floors. Matched with the wood panelling on the walls, lined with portraits of famous people, it felt more like an art gallery than a school hall.

Jess walked past paintings of the Brontë's, Joseph Priestley, John Foster, Samson Fox and Thomas Fairfax. These were people from Yorkshire, there to inspire the current pupils, as they looked down upon them. Jess imagined the feeling of privilege you might get from going to a school that was beautiful in its own right. No one thought that way about the school in the shabbier state in which they knew it. Most would moan about having to go there every day and couldn't wait until they were allowed to leave.

Outside, without the dining hall and sports block, the school was no bigger than a large primary school and it was fascinating to the children to think so few pupils attended. Many buildings in the area dated back to Victorian times and had been built using Yorkshire Stone, with Hickley School being no exception. In the present day, the outsides of these buildings had turned black due to many years of pollution.

However, here they were, looking at walls the colour of golden sand and rather than being a blot on the landscape, the school was a beacon of light, glowing in the winter sunshine. Even the rows of terraced mill-worker cottages that lined the streets opposite the school were less black than they were used to and it made the area so much prettier. Walking the cobbled streets around the outside of the school, some of it was recognisable; the rest was all farmland.

"It's weird to think none of these farms exists now," Jess said.

"I know. I kind of like it like this," Nadia said.

Jess agreed. It was much nicer to see all that green space rather than built-up housing developments. When they re-joined Tomma and Ash, the girls told them about their lessons that morning and how difficult they'd found them.

"I don't like the sound of that. Do we have to go back to

school this afternoon?" Ash said. "Why don't we see if we can get a train home now?"

"Now you want to go!" Jess said. It was only the thought of lessons that would put Ash off being stuck in a time-warp. "We'll have to get on the last carriage again." She was convinced that was where the magic happened.

They decided to go and see. As the four of them walked in silence to the train station, they were neither in a hurry nor taking their time, but seemed to fall in to step with each other. Together, as one unit, they were stronger, but even so, Jess could sense the nervous tension crackling in the air around them. She noticed for the first time how different they were to the strangers they passed in the street and it made the feeling of intruding on another world stronger; like listening in to a conversation, or spying from another room.

As she looked around at the women dressed in smart suits, nipped in at the waist and with matching hats, like clones of each other. They reminded her of ants getting on with their day. There were more women than men; the only men there presumably being the ones who were too old or unable to go off to war.

Jess realised these people were going to experience things that only she and her friends knew about—things that hadn't even happened yet. It made her feel all-knowing, with power over them that she didn't want, and it caused her grip on Nadia to tighten. Jess sped up a little. The urgency to get home, back to familiarity, grew stronger as they neared the station.

In the same way that they hadn't taken the time to notice what was going on around them earlier that morning, not one of them had appreciated how lovely Hickley station was.

It was so different from what they were used to. The waiting room was clean, for a start. In place of the split and broken plastic seats were rows of red velvet-lined benches. There was also a tearoom to one side and a lit coal fire giving warmth to the room, as well as lighting it with its orange glow. The place was empty though, which Jess thought was not a good sign.

As the children stepped into the waiting room, the first thing they all did was to automatically look up for the timetable, before realising there would be no screen. Instead, there was a woman stood on a small stepladder sliding out white metal squares on which were written the letters and numbers that put together, indicated the destinations and times of the trains.

"Excuse me," Tomma said, walking up to her and standing patiently by the ladder.

She stopped and turned around, smiling down warmly at him.

"When's the next train to Kirkshaw, please?"

"Kirkshaw? Next one doesn't come until four," she said, then noticing the disappointment on the faces, she stepped down and turned to face them. She was wearing what looked like a guard's uniform, but with a skirt rather than trousers. The skirt wasn't as long as those of the women they'd seen in the streets. It came to mid-calf length and the rest of her legs were covered with boots that came up to the knee. Her hair was all hidden inside a hat, which looked like it was made for someone with a much bigger head than hers.

"Didn't you know we only have one coming in on a morning and one leaving at the end of the day? We're running a reduced service as we're short of drivers," she said. "Been learning how to drive one myself. Hoping to pass my test next week."

The woman looked pleased about that and it was obvious she loved her job, but it didn't help the children and no one knew what to say to her. They turned slowly to leave, heads down and shoulders slumped. Jess was trying hard not to cry.

"So, that's it then," Nadia said when they were back outside. "We have to go back to school and suffer lessons for the afternoon. I don't think I can stand it."

"Me neither," Ash said.

"You didn't even do lessons this morning," Jess said. "You were outside digging up potatoes."

"I know, but if they're anything like you said, I don't want to go. It makes our lessons seem easy and fun in comparison, which coming from me is saying something," Ash said.

Ash had a point. Even though he hadn't experienced what the lessons were like yet, he was already under the impression it would be a lot worse than what they were used to and he was right about that. Jess didn't spend her days at school feeling terrified to speak or get anything wrong. She didn't have to sit in silence the whole time, and the teachers were like angels compared with what they had come across so far. AND they had pens, proper ones that actually worked, AND computers, AND of course, they had Instagram.

Chapter 10

If You Can't Beat 'Em, Join 'Em

It was a slow trudge back up the hill towards the school. A cloud of defeat hung directly above them, dampening all hopes of getting home sooner rather than later, or even if they were going to ever get home at all. They just didn't know, but at least they knew there would be a train going to Kirkshaw later, so they could at least try.

After discussing whether to hide out until four, they decided it was too cold and they had nowhere to go and nothing to do. School seemed like the better option. As they neared the building, they joined other pupils heading from home back for afternoon lessons. The pupils were chatting, messing about, pushing each other around and acting in much the same way as Jess and her school colleagues usually did.

Jess wasn't sure why that surprised her, but given there was a war on, she thought they would all be miserable. It didn't seem that way at all. Life just seemed normal.

Remembering the split of pupils in the playgrounds, Jess and Nadia said goodbye to Tomma and Ash at the corner of the road, arranging to meet them at the same spot at home time.

"Good luck," Jess said, feeling reluctant to let them leave. It wasn't the same having lessons without her close friends around her, especially Tomma.

"Let's get on with this, then," Nadia said. "I wonder if Martha is back yet. She was nice, wasn't she? It was like she was the only one who noticed us. The others don't seem to care."

"I'm sure they have more important things to think about," Jess said. "And Martha said they were used to new people coming. She said something about bombings. I didn't know we were bombed in World War I, did you?"

Before Nadia could answer, the bell rang out and this time, the girls knew to line up. They found Martha and huddled together with her at the back of the line.

"Thanks for your help this morning, Martha," Jess said. "We felt a bit silly not knowing what to do."

"That's all right. Everybody keeps away from the new 'uns these days. They don't want to be reminded of their own fathers and brothers who are missing or dead."

Martha's hair was hanging loosely across her right shoulder and she fiddled with the ends as she spoke. The bright auburn tones did not go with the brown uniform and it reminded Jess how much she hated wearing those colours too. Who thought a brown uniform was a good idea? It must have been the school's colours right from the start and was quite possibly designed to make you look as plain as possible. If you had red hair though, it was even worse.

"It must be hard," said Jess, trying to bring her focus back to the real issues at hand.

"My mamma's not slept for weeks. Dad's recovering in

hospital, but until he's home, she won't rest. Then there's Henry still in France. We haven't heard anything so we're all worried sick. I just wish this whole thing was over."

Jess and Nadia looked at each other, both guilt-ridden and neither knowing what to say. Martha could sense their awkwardness and her face broke into a smile.

"I hope you're ready for Games," she said, rubbing her gloved hands together as if warming up already.

"Games?" Nadia and Jess said at the same time.

"As in PE?" Nadia asked raising her eyebrows.

"What's PE?" Martha frowned.

"Oh, never mind, sorry," Nadia said, turning to Jess and whispering, "Awkward." Nadia put her face into her hands and groaned. "You know what this means?"

Jess didn't know what she meant and looked at Nadia questioningly.

"No kit," Nadia said, nudging her. Now it was Jess's turn to groan. It was the thought of another telling off and another visit to Matron.

"Just come in for register, then when everyone goes to the changing rooms to get ready, you can sneak off to Matron then," Martha said, as though it was obvious. "That way no one will realise you don't have your things."

"Good idea," Jess said.

They lined up behind the others, falling silent as they filed towards the classroom. Jess was already beginning to get nervous again and could feel her stomach churning. She hated PE at the best of times.

*

Miss Jennings was sitting at her desk and she peered at them over the top of her glasses as they all scuttled into the classroom, eager to get to their seats. One look from her was all it took to say this was a no-nonsense, get-on-with-it affair. Jess took her seat at the back of the room, next to Martha.

"Silence, girls," the teacher said, even though no one was speaking. "Please gather your things and proceed to the changing rooms."

Martha gave Jess a nod. This was their opportunity to sneak away to Matron's office for yet another uniform change. Jess wondered how bad the PE kit would be. They ran across the hall and out the door behind the main office, which came out just across from the annexe building where the sick room was.

Matron looked up from her desk in confusion, as they bumbled in through the door, eager to get in and out before anyone noticed.

"Back again so soon, ladies?" she said.

"We need PE—I mean games kits," Nadia said, whilst Jess could only look down at the floor in embarrassment.

Although Matron only raised her eyebrows and looked a little irritated at being disturbed from her paperwork, she didn't question why they didn't have the right things with them. She went to her cupboard, took out some shorts and cotton tops and handed them over.

"Try these on. I think they will be the right size for you," Matron said, without even looking at either of them.

The girls took the garments from her, nodding their thanks before looking at them and then at each other. The shorts were a brown cotton material, long and baggy. They came down to the knees, looking more like culottes than shorts. The tops were equally as baggy, like shirts, or even an old-fashioned pyjama top. They were awful, truly awful, but Nadia, of course, still found it hilarious.

"Shut up," Jess said, pushing past her. "Come on, we're not supposed to be here, are we?"

Complete with plimsolls, also borrowed from Matron's lost property box, they squeaked their way back across the yard just as the other girls were coming out of the changing rooms. Martha smiled and waved at them to join her in the line, but not before they had thrown their uniform into the changing room along with everybody else's. It seemed everything at school involved standing or moving in a line. Jess wondered how they would manage to do any PE if they weren't allowed to move from that formation.

Whilst they had been changing, Miss Jennings and some of the other girls had transformed the main hall into a playing court, fastening nets across each side. Relieved they weren't going out into the cold Jess began to relax a little.

"Yes! It's badminton," Nadia said, elbowing Jess lightly in the ribs and nodding towards the rackets and shuttlecocks on the floor at the side.

As they took up their positions, Jess noticed the boys hard at work in their classroom, which was off the main hall like theirs but on the opposite side. It looked as though they were having a maths lesson, from what she could see on the blackboard. Tomma had his head down, bent over his desk, concentrating hard. Ash was shaking the quill pen in frustration and some of the ink splashed on to his face, making him jump. Jess couldn't help laughing. She knew the boys would hate their afternoon and felt guilty that hers was going to be much more fun.

The boys' teacher seemed to shout a lot more than Miss Jennings did. He was booming at them constantly, enough to make Jess jump too, even though she was nowhere near. She turned her attention to the badminton with Nadia instead and they got into a rhythm. The rackets were much heavier than they were used to, as were the shuttlecocks but they managed to hold together a few rallies.

Chapter 11

Trying To Get Home

"What happens now?" Jess said to Martha, as they changed back into their uniforms.

"What do you mean?" she said and stopped to look at them. It was as if she was seeing them for the first time. "Is school so different where you're from?"

Jess felt her face heat up and looked at Nadia, hoping she would come to her rescue.

"We never have Games at the end of the day, so we were just wondering if we have to go back to class or if we can leave when the bell goes," Nadia said. She was always good at thinking on her feet and had gotten the pair of them out of many a scrape. Jess, on the other hand, couldn't lie to save her life.

"Oh, well we have to go back to class for home time prayers," Martha said. "Then we wait to be dismissed."

Both Jess and Nadia were disappointed they couldn't just escape. They were itching to get home, or at least down to the station to see if they could catch the right train. Feeling suddenly drained after the energy rush of the afternoon's exercise, they followed Martha, somewhat dejectedly, in the line again, back to class, where Miss Jennings was waiting. She didn't look like she had moved, even though she had been walking around the hall observing the girls' badminton skills.

The home time prayer was the Lord's Prayer, which was a relief for Jess because she knew it off by heart. Then the sound of a bell coming from the hall, and the way the other girls began to fidget, signalled it was time to go home. The children had survived a day in First World War Hickley School and all they had to do now was get back to the present day. Easy if you knew how.

"Class, you may be dismissed," Miss Jennings said and there followed a collective sigh of relief. It seemed they weren't the only ones eager to get away.

"See you on Monday," Martha said as she shut away her things in the desk and got up to put on her coat.

Jess could only smile weakly at her, not wanting to say how it was unlikely they would ever see each other again. Jess hung back and watched her go before moving down towards Nadia.

"Let's go home," Nadia said, linking arms.

Jess crossed fingers on both hands and held them up. She didn't trust herself to speak at that moment. Together, they walked towards the corner of the street to where they'd parted from Tomma and Ash after lunch.

"Please let there be that magic last carriage," Jess said when they had greeted the boys.

"Don't worry, it will be there," Tomma said confidently. "I'm sure of it."

Just as Tomma was sure of most things, he was sure of this too. Jess wished she had his faith. She clutched tighter to Nadia. The anticipation and worry of whether they would be able to get the train and make it home, made Jess so nervous she couldn't speak.

Ash clearly didn't feel the same. He chatted non-stop about his afternoon as they walked down the hill towards the station, among the crowds of other pupils making their way home too.

"Having Crawford for maths was torture," Ash said. "He didn't explain what you had to do. He just turned to the board and scratched his way through some seriously complicated calculations, muttering what could have been Chinese for all I know. Didn't understand a word. Saw what you were wearing though. That was hilarious. Almost laughed out loud, I did, but Crawford would have gone ballistic. You weren't even allowed to fart in there."

It all came out in one breath and Nadia burst out laughing.

"Ash, have you ever had to be silent for that long? It must have killed you," Nadia said.

"Oh, it did, almost, but wait 'til you hear about what else we learned. It was awesome. Tell 'em, Tomma."

The girls turned to look at Tomma, whose face broke into a big smile.

"Science," he said, looking smug.

"Science? Well, that sounds really interesting. . . not," Nadia rolled her eyes.

"But not just normal boring science," Ash said, and he was jumping up and down by now, his excitement getting the better of him.

Tomma sighed. "Why don't you just tell them?" Tomma looked at Ash, who seemed about to burst.

"It was all about the science of grenades and other bombs

they've been using in this war," Ash said, blurting out the words in his excitement. "Crawford told us about all the different ones that have been developed, how they work and about the factories that make them. There's one in Leeds and it's mostly women who work there. They have yellow-stained fingers and faces because of the chemicals they use. People call them little canaries."

"Go the women!" Nadia said, punching the air with her fist.

"This was what Crawford said, and I quote. . ." Ash stopped walking and the others had to stop and turn towards him. He cleared his throat and puffed out his chest in readiness for his impression of Mr Crawford. "You see, that's the thing about war. It forces many new developments in order to keep up with the enemy. Whatever the Germans make, we try to do one better. It keeps us on our toes and it makes sure we stay one step ahead of them. That's how we are winning this war, gentlemen."

It was so over-the-top, even Jess had to laugh.

*

At the station, the children went to the platform and waited for the train. There were a few other school children already there, as well as a lady with little ones running in circles around her and a couple of old men, sitting on a bench smoking their pipes. Other than that, it was quiet for the time of day, but when the train arrived, it cut through the quiet with a rip-roaring screech as it came to a halt. A cloud of black smoke enveloped the platform and, desperate to make sure they got on the last carriage, but unable to see in the dense, choking smog, the children had to fight their way through, holding their breath.

The train seemed unusually long and it took a few minutes to walk to the end. Not surprisingly, no one else had bothered to walk that far, so the four of them were alone in the carriage as they had been that morning. They all sighed when the train began to move slowly away.

"Well, every carriage looks exactly the same, so I hope this is the right one," Jess said. As before, they were in a carriage that had a compartment off a narrow corridor, with two, carpeted bench seats opposite each other.

"Try not to worry, Jess, I'm sure it will be fine," Nadia said, dumping her bag on the floor and making herself comfortable on the seat.

As the train moved off, the landscape changed from industrial buildings and mills, alive with activity, smoke pluming from their tall chimneys, to field after field, separated by dry-stone walls and filled with grazing sheep as they left the town behind. Usually, the landscape whizzed by in a blur and it wasn't possible to appreciate it. The sheer emptiness was fascinating. There were so fewer houses back then, but as Jess stared out of the window, her view suddenly became obscured by a cloud of smoke billowing past and almost seeming to hug itself against the train. Jess withdrew, holding her nose to escape the now-familiar smell.

When the smoke cleared, the train seemed to be moving much faster than it had been and when she looked out of the window again, it wasn't so easy to make out the landscape this time. Concentrating harder, Jess noticed the world outside had changed too.

"Look," she said, jumping up and straining to see if what she thought was happening was true. The others stood and joined her at the window. "Does it look different to you? More buildings. . . and there's a car over there, a proper one. I mean modern."

Her heart sped up as the train whizzed over a road, where there was a petrol station. Never had the sight of such a dull and nondescript landmark been so welcoming.

"I think we're back!"

Everyone gave a whoop and the boys high-fived each other, the tension seeming to have lifted and blown away along with the rest of the smoke. As the train came to a stop, Jess watched with joy as it pulled alongside the run-down station building of Kirkshaw, with its familiar peeling, painted-wood walls, covered with graffiti. The station building itself was no more than an empty shell, apart from the one-person ticket office that had a few broken plastic chairs. Jess never thought she would be so relieved to see the horrible old place again.

They stepped off the train and watched as it pulled away out of sight, marvelling at its magnificence, whilst at the same time wondering how on earth it had managed to take them back in time. It all seemed so crazy.

"I don't think we should tell anyone about today," Nadia said as if answering all their thoughts. "They'll think we've gone mad."

"What if they find out we weren't at school?" said Jess.

"We'll worry about that later," Ash said, even though he knew if his parents found out he'd skipped school he would be in trouble, big time.

"Listen, does anyone want to meet up tomorrow to try and work out what went on today? I want to know the actual year we landed in and why," Tomma said. His curiosity and need-to-know nature would not be satisfied until he had answers. Tomma found he could usually find the answers to most things if he looked hard enough.

Everyone agreed, except Jess, who ignored the shaking of heads and disapproving looks. Jess at that moment was happy enough to be back home to the normal world and time. She would have been quite content to hide under her duvet, never to emerge again, rather than dig into why they had travelled back in time.

"Come on, Jess! It won't be the same without you," Tomma said.

It was the sound of the old Tomma. The one who had always been by her side, but hadn't been so much as of late. It was as if he'd been caught off-guard and had almost forgotten himself. As Jess looked at him, he blushed, causing a flush of heat to her own cheeks.

"Oh, all right then," she said, resigning herself to the fact they were in this together. She had to admit she did want to know—there was at least one curious bone in her body! But she wasn't about to tell them that. And the fact Tomma had asked her, well. . .

"Cool." Tomma said. "Mum and Dad are out in the morning, so why don't you come to mine and we'll see what we can find out? At least no one will be nosing around wondering what we're doing. If they come back early, we can tell them it's a school project."

"I can't wait to get home now," Ash said. "I'm starving."

"We'd better get changed out of this disgusting uniform first though before anyone starts asking questions," Nadia said, looking at Jess, who in turn looked down at her clothes and laughed. She had completely forgotten she was wearing it. Nadia linked arms with her. "Come on, we can change at mine. No one will be home yet."

Chapter 12

History In The Making

The shock of the previous day's events had wiped Jess out, making it a struggle getting up early the next day. She usually didn't rise much before ten on a weekend, but Tomma said his house would only be empty in the morning, so they'd agreed to meet at nine. She thought about not turning up and letting the others do all the research, but her conscience got the better of her. Unable to sleep any longer, she got up, cursing that annoying voice in her head for always thinking it knew better.

Jess was downstairs, fully dressed and eating breakfast by the time her mum came into the kitchen, bleary-eyed and with her hair sticking up in all directions. She stopped short when she saw Jess.

"Yes, you are seeing correctly. I am up and I am dressed even though it's a Saturday morning," Jess said.

With her mum's mouth moving, but nothing coming out, Jess thought it would be easier if she just said everything it looked like she was thinking. Her mum shook her head in disbelief and went to put the kettle on.

"Where are you off to so early, then?" her mum asked as

she came to sit down opposite Jess, nursing her mug of tea in her hands.

"I'm going to Tomma's to work on a school project. Nadia and Ash will be there too. He hasn't got any other time except this morning." Jess blushed as she spoke and looked down into her bowl of cereal to hide her face, wondering why saying she was babbling so much about going to Tomma's house.

The thought of Tomma made her heart speed up a little. It happened every time she was around him and Jess couldn't look directly at her mum, knowing she would see straight through her. She wasn't ready to start answering questions about boys just yet.

"What's the project about?"

"Oh, it's just. . . stuff," Jess said, stacking the little circular O's of her cereal up on top of one another.

"Of course, stuff, yes, I know that one. Well, you should make sure you get all your homework out of the way before that big sleepover at school on Monday. God knows what they were thinking of having all the Year Sevens overnight at the school. They must be crazy. You'll be fit for nothing for the rest of the week."

Jess looked up. She'd forgotten all about the sleepover. Their year group were staying at school for the night. It was supposed to be a bonding thing.

"I hope they're going to put the boys separate from the girls," her mum said.

Jess blushed. "Mum, don't be ridiculous, it's not like that."

Her mum didn't look convinced as she got up, putting her mug in the sink. "Anyway, I'm off for a shower. Have fun today." She kissed Jess on the top of her head and shuffled away in her over-sized slippers.

Jess held up the bowl to her mouth and drank the milk left at the bottom before heading off to the bathroom to brush her teeth and finish getting ready. Tomma's house was opposite Nadia's and just around the corner from Ash. They all lived on the other side of the village to Jess, but it wasn't far.

She picked up her school bag, thinking she should take it with her for authenticity's sake and as she wrapped up in hat, scarf and gloves, Jess thought about Martha Stenchion. *Was it as cold for Martha that day as it was for her? Did she have enough clothes to keep her warm or enough fuel for her fire?* Jess wondered if her family had eaten that morning and if they'd had any news about her brother. Martha had been so worried because they hadn't heard anything from him. It must have been very difficult living at that time.

*

Ash was jumping up and down like an excited puppy when he opened the door to let Jess in. She took off her coat and hung it up on the hooks by the front door, along with the hat, scarf and gloves. She went to join Tomma and Ash in the study.

Jess loved Tomma's house. It was Victorian, with a big front door that had a stained-glass panel at the top of it. The door opened into a wide hall, tiled with small squares that were like a chessboard, and when the sun was shining, the light from the window reflected off the coloured glass and bounced about the squares as if it were dancing. Tomma's dad's study had one wall lined ceiling to floor, almost, with dark wooden shelves, all filled with books. In front of the huge bay window was an enormous mahogany desk, a deep red-brown wood, which always made her think of conkers. The desk was topped with brown leather and edged with gold. It was truly beautiful. It was also so huge everyone could fit around it.

Tomma and Ash had brought in chairs from the dining room and Jess went to sit on the one to Tomma's right, giving him a shy smile and trying to ignore the way being so close to him felt. Nadia arrived and they gathered around the enormous flat-screen monitor of the computer.

"Okay this is the weird thing," Nadia said, as she sat down, holding her hands up and towards the others to get their attention. They turned to look at her. "I phoned Jane last night and asked her was there anything strange about us yesterday. I wanted to find out whether we were going to get into trouble for not being at school, right?"

The others nodded.

"Well, she asked what I meant and I asked did she see me? She thought was weird but she said that she did. Then she stopped because actually, she just didn't really remember noticing me at all, but she said there was no one missing off the register, so we must have been there. And then she had a go at me because I think everybody should always be looking at me and giving me attention, which of course is not true and not the reason why I was asking all this, is it?"

She looked intently at the others, who realising they were supposed to react, all starting nodding vigorously at once and expressing that of course it wasn't and that no, Nadia was not vain. Jess turned to the boys. Ash was pulling a funny face and shaking his head. Tomma stared deep in thought at an unidentifiable spot on the desktop. He looked up.

"So, we were marked on the register as being at school, because effectively, we were there, just not in the same time zone. Ash, you're good at science, got anything to offer by way of explanation?" Tomma asked.

"I haven't got a clue, mate," Ash said, scratching his head. "It's not as if time travel is actually a thing you study in physics, is it? It just seems like we were there, yet we weren't there, as though we were in two time zones at the same time."

"Yeah, Ash, that makes loads of sense, thanks for that." Nadia laughed.

"Like a parallel universe," Tomma said. "You can't be in two places at the same time though, can you?"

"We weren't though," Jess said. "It's like what Mrs Kennedy was saying the other day. about the ghosts of the past live within these walls. So, when we're at school, normally all the pupils of the past are there with us, but in spirit. When *we* went back to the past yesterday, we were still there in the present, but this time, it was our spirit that was there, not our actual bodies. And the school recognised our presence, so no one needed to be alerted to our absence. It's easy to blend in unnoticed when there are so many other pupils to think about. Half the teachers don't even know we exist anyway."

"It explains why our parents didn't get a call to find out why we weren't at school," Nadia said. She turned to look at the computer screen. "So, what did you find out? Anything?"

Jess was still focused on the idea of existing across more

than one time. It was hard enough just getting your head around the fact they'd even gone back in time at all. She wondered how Nadia could be so matter-of-fact about it.

"I was just about to show you before you dropped that bombshell," Tomma said, as he turned his attention back to the monitor. "Remember that guy in assembly? He said something about the Allies making a peace treaty, yeah? Well, we realised that Monday coming is Remembrance Day. That's the day the First World War ended."

"Yeah," Ash said, cutting in. "That's the day the Allies signed that peace thingy and agreed to end the war. We reckon that's what the fella was talking about."

"If that's right, it means we definitely went back in time to 1918," Nadia said. "The First World War lasted from 1914 to 1918, didn't it? You reckon Monday is 11th November 1918?"

Tomma and Ash nodded, both looking pleased.

"What do you think, Jess?" Nadia said.

Everyone looked at her, which made her squirm. She didn't like this sort of attention and could feel a blush spreading across her face.

"Well," she said, with some hesitation. "It *is* the centenary, which might explain why we went back there."

"It doesn't explain why *us* though," Nadia said. "Why were we picked to go there? Who picked us and how was it possible? What does it all mean?"

No one had any answers, so they spent the morning looking up details about their school, finding the date when it first opened and photos through the years. As they looked through them, they recognised the original buildings they'd seen first-hand.

"Look, Mr Fothergill was the first Headmaster. That's him, isn't it?" Jess said, pointing to the screen.

Sure enough, a familiar bearded man wearing a long-tailed suit complete with pocket watch stared back at them. Underneath the photo was a paragraph explaining that Mr Fothergill was Headmaster from 1898, when the school first opened, to 1923. He was particularly proud of the Old Boys who served and died in the Great War, regularly reading out their letters sending news from the trenches. In 1920, he unveiled the war memorial engraved with the names of the ninety-three ex-pupils killed in the war. What stood out for Jess was a statement Mr Fothergill made at that time:

'The war has touched the lives of many, not least the pupils of this school following the deaths of some of our own. These boys may not have been known by many of the present scholars, but the staff and many of the Old Boys and Old Girls felt a keen and personal loss when the news of their deaths reached the school.

We are proud to know them and that they died so well and for so great a cause. These young men entered the war from a sense of duty, knowing the risk of great misfortune or of death, yet they chose the path of a true man. His fellows may rejoice in his choice, even though they are called upon to mourn his death.'

Mr Fothergill had wanted Hickley School pupils to remember the fallen and have something to remind them of what those boys had sacrificed for the sake of their country. Jess thought about Martha's brother and wondered if had he survived.

"It says here that on Armistice Day all the schools let

everyone out early and there were street parties and celebrations all over the place," Ash said. "I bet that was so cool."

"Yeah, can you imagine what it would have been like that day, to know the war was finally over and we'd won?" Tomma said. Then his expression darkened. "Having said that, my mum was part of a war, but she never seems to celebrate the fact that Croatia won."

"I don't imagine it always feels that way for the ordinary people," Jess said. "All they see is death and loss and for what?"

"We should go back to witness that if we can, though," Ash said.

"I'd be up for that. Are you in?" Tomma said to Nadia and Jess.

Nadia looked at Jess's uncertain face. "Come on, Jess, it would be amazing. How often do you get to see history in the making or even history that's already been made? I mean, it's surreal. We're talking about going back in time to witness the end of the First World War."

Jess felt a bubbling of excitement inside her. Nadia was right. What an amazing opportunity—and one they would be stupid to pass up.

"Let's do it," she said with a squeal. Her smile then faded as she suddenly felt unsure. "What if we go there and we can't get back this time though?"

Everyone groaned.

"Oh, come on, live a little for once," Tomma said.

Jess glared at him, slightly hurt by his accusation. His face seemed to soften, though, as he picked up her hand and wrapped it in both of his. Jess felt as though she might stop breathing.

"Whatever happens, we'll find a way to deal with it and we'll stick together, okay?" he said, looking directly at her. He was so sure and confident Jess felt that confidence flow through his hands and into hers too.

"Okay," she said, nodding softly at him, the beginnings of a smile creeping across her face. "I'm in."

"Yay! I'm so glad," Nadia said. "We wouldn't want to go without you."

Jess glared at her. "You would go without me, then?"

Judging by how bright red Nadia's face became, Jess took that as a yes. That thought irritated her for about a second until she realised, she couldn't blame them if they wanted to go and she didn't. It wouldn't be fair of her to stop them.

"Well, good job I'm coming then, isn't it? There's something I need to do first, though. I'll catch up with you later."

Nadia looked as though she wanted to interrogate, but thought better of it. Jess wasn't trying to be secretive, but with thoughts of Martha and her family on her mind, there was something she needed to do—alone.

Chapter 13

Searching For Henry

As Jess stepped into her house, she met her mum, who was just coming down the stairs.

"Did you get everything done at Tomma's?" she said.

"Yep," Jess said, diving into the shoe cupboard so she could avoid looking at her mum and praying she wouldn't ask about what they had been up to. "Oh actually, I didn't quite." Remembering there was something else she wanted to do, Jess turned around and backed out of the cupboard. "Are you going into town by any chance? I could do with a lift."

"I am, as it happens," her mum replied. "Just about to go in a minute, if you're ready."

"Great," Jess said, going back into the cupboard to retrieve the shoes she had just kicked off when she was in there. "Hope this isn't going to be as crazy a ride as yesterday."

"Cheeky," her mum said, giving Jess a wry smile as she pushed her gently ahead and out the door.

*

Jess asked her mum to drop her at Hickley School and they

arranged to meet in the town centre, which was just down the road, so she could get a lift home. After waving her mum off, she turned to stare at the school, taking in the details. The soot-stained stone building—the original part of the school—now had the familiar dining hall attached to it. There were classrooms above the dining room, the windows of which were tall with a rounded top.

To the left of this was the DT room and to the right, across the yard was the sports block, the more modern, Sixties-style, ugly building that didn't match the original. Although it was all so familiar to Jess, today, it seemed as though she were looking at it for the first time.

The school's sports centre opened to the public at weekends, which meant the school was usually open too. Jess wasn't interested in the sports hall though and instead, headed away from it, towards the main school building. She stopped as she recalled Mr Crawford marching her and Nadia through the same corridor the previous day, sending them towards the girls' yard on the other side of the building. She walked down the corridor to the foyer at the end. This was the entrance hub to the school, the first bit a visitor would see if they came to visit.

Glancing around, Jess found what she was looking for: the war memorial tucked away on the far side of the wall. She walked up to it and, as she looked at the list of names, kept her fingers crossed.

"Henry Stenchion, Henry Stenchion. . ." Jess repeated to herself as she scanned the names, touching the embossed writing with the tip of her finger.

Jess held her breath, hoping she wouldn't find Martha's

brother on the list and when his name wasn't there she breathed out in relief.

Thank God for that, Jess thought. He must have survived the war.

She looked at the other names from the First World War years. They were the Hickley Old Boys, whom the Headmaster, Mr Fothergill, had referred to in assembly. For the first time, Jess saw them as real people rather than just names: someone's brother, nephew or son. She felt their loss.

On the way back to meet her mum, Jess wondered how she was going to explain to Martha that her brother would make it safely through the war. Why would Martha believe she was being anything other than kind and positive in order to keep her spirits up? Jess felt she owed it to Martha somehow, but wasn't sure why. Perhaps it was because Martha was the only person who'd bothered to help them when they'd arrived at Hickley School in 1918. No one else seemed to care, probably too preoccupied with their own lives, but Martha was different. Despite all her worries, she'd gone out of her way to be helpful and kind. And there was something about her Jess was drawn to. Even though they'd only met for the first time, Jess felt as though she'd known Martha all her life.

Chapter 14

Re-Tracing Steps

Monday morning came around and Jess woke to the sound of the alarm on her mobile. As a precaution, she'd set a second alarm, so she wouldn't have to go through the same drama as she had done on Friday. They'd had another power cut, which she knew (or at least had hoped) was the first step if they were going to get back in time again. She looked at her radio alarm clock. Once again it flashed 03:42 and that caused a flutter to rush through her body. She got up, knowing she needed to prepare herself mentally for the day to come. The house was quiet and everyone else had slept through, so she went to each room to wake them and let them know.

Despite her nerves, Jess was at least grateful for the chance to get up at her normal time, have breakfast and prepare for school without the panicky madness that had been Friday. Today was also the day of the big sleepover, so she needed to be extra prepared. She put her overnight things in a rucksack and went to retrieve a sleeping bag from the airing cupboard before going downstairs. It struck Jess as strange that her day would involve experiencing Hickley School in two very different ways, one in wartime 1918 and the other for a crazy Year Seven sleepover.

"Have you got everything you need for tonight? Sleeping bag, toothbrush, fresh pants?" Jess's mum said as they were eating breakfast.

Jess raised her eyebrows. "Yes, thanks. I know how to pack for a sleepover."

"All right, sarky! Are you looking forward to it?"

"Not really. It's going to be manic and I hate sleeping on the floor."

"Is that why you're being so ratty then? We've got a camping mat in the garage, you know? You should take that. It will make it a bit warmer as well."

Jess had been dreading the school sleepover. It was something the Year Sevens did every year as part of the school's 'let's get to know each other' activities. Jess thought it was the worst way to get to know the other kids in the year. Who wants to see sleepy-eyed, scruffy-haired kids first thing in the morning after having virtually no sleep? It wasn't her idea of fun, but Nadia had convinced her to go and she didn't want to let her down. Ash would be going to it too, and Tomma. . .

She blushed at the thought and told herself off for always doing that, then quickly pushed whatever thoughts she had to the back of her mind. She got up to tidy away her breakfast things.

"Here you go, found it." Her mum put the sleeping mat down on the floor. "You'd better get the rest of your stuff and be on your way. Can you carry this lot to the station or do you want a lift?"

"Thanks, Mum and sorry," Jess said. She went over to her

mum and threw her arms around her waist. Sometimes, she still felt like she needed a cuddle from her mum. Her mum squeezed her tight.

"Lift? Me, please," Declan said, as he came into the kitchen. He let his over-sized sports bag drop to the floor with a loud thump before crashing and banging his way around the kitchen getting breakfast.

Their mum laughed. "Bull, china shop," she said, shaking her head as she turned to leave the room. "Be ready in five, you two."

As Jess sat in the car on the way to the station, she felt the flutter of nerves jangling around in her stomach along to the rhythm of the car's engine. A part of her hoped there wouldn't be a mysterious steam carriage at the back of their train. Another part of her wanted to go back to see Martha again. She needed to tell her that her brother would come home safely from the trenches. Martha needed to have something to hope for.

The children had agreed they would arrive late to the station as they had done on Friday morning as if that had somehow contributed to them getting on the magical carriage, but by getting a lift, Jess had ended up being early. She said goodbye to her brother, saying she would wait for her friends outside. Declan was halfway up the stairs before she'd even finished speaking.

The others arrived together, with one minute to spare, breathless from carrying their heavy loads.

"You been here a while?" Tomma said as he set his rucksack down as if it was the lightest thing in the world.

"I got a lift," Jess said.

"All right for some. Right, are we doing this, then?" he said, looking at the three of them and rubbing his hands together in readiness.

"Defo," said Ash. "Let's cut down through that hedge again, exactly the same as we did on Friday."

They all had their own ideas about what made the magic work.

"We agreed we'd wait for the train to come in first, then make a run for it, didn't we?" Nadia said.

"Yeah but we should at least go up to the top of the bridge," Jess said. "With all these extra bags today, it will make us a bit slower. Well, me anyway. We didn't think about that bit."

"Yeah, Jess is right, come on," Tomma said, picking up his rucksack and leading the way. "I can hear the announcement. The train's coming."

The four of them retraced their steps and made it to the far end of the platform as the train pulled into the station.

"There it is," Nadia said, pointing to the last carriage. Before them, was an ordinary diesel train with electric sliding doors, scruffy, nondescript and functional, but with a beautiful steam train carriage attached at the end.

"Why have we never noticed this before?" Jess said, looking around to see if anyone else was about to head that way. No one did though.

"Never mind that, get over there quick!" Ash said, shoving her along with a gentle push.

Tomma opened the door and threw his bag on first, grabbing Jess's and doing the same. He tried to take Nadia's, but she resisted, stepping aboard with it held firmly in front of her. Jess stepped in after Ash, with Tomma the last in. He pulled the heavy door shut with a loud click just as the whistle blew.

"We did it!" said Tomma, flopping down into the seat. "We're about to witness one of the most important days in our history."

Chapter 15

Bittersweet Celebrations

"Have you got your uniform?" Nadia said, as the train picked up speed and began to settle into a steady rhythm.

"It should be in the bottom of my bag from Friday," Jess said as she rummaged around. "Here it is. Yuck! I forgot how ugly it was."

Tomma laughed. "You both looked hilarious wearing those," he said.

"Shut up," said Jess, shoving him in the chest.

"Anyway, you need to get out so we can change," Nadia said, shooing them away with her hand.

"Go out where?" said Ash.

"The corridor, of course, and no peeping," Nadia said, ushering the boys out of the seating compartment and into the tiny corridor before they had time to protest. She closed the door and pulled down the blind. "That's handy. They won't be able to see in now."

As the girls changed, they couldn't help but giggle at each other. It all seemed so ridiculous. Then there was a knock on the door.

"Can we come in now?" Tomma said.

Nadia let the blind back up with a snap and slid open the door. "Not a word," she said, giving the boys a stern look as they came back in to sit down.

It was obvious each of them was trying not to laugh, but neither was going to break first and suffer the wrath of Nadia.

*

"What're we going to do with all our stuff?" Ash said when they arrived at school. The air was crisp and there was a touch of frost on the ground, but they were warm after lugging their heavy loads up the hill. "We can't carry these rucksacks around all day."

"Yeah, we look like we're going on a camping trip," Jess said.

"What about the music room?" Nadia pointed to a small stone hut at the far side of the main building. It was out of the way and not many people used it, so they agreed their things would be safe there.

"It's a coal store," Tomma said when they opened the door and looked inside. "Bit dirty."

"Yeah, well at least no-one is likely to come in and steal our stuff," Ash said.

There wasn't much coal in there anyway, another reminder of how hard the times were. They put their rucksacks and sleeping bags together on one side, as far away from the coal pile as possible, then split up to go to their respective yards. When the girls walked over to theirs, they spotted Martha's auburn hair straight away and went to join her.

"Hi, Martha, did you have a good weekend?" Nadia said.

"As well as can be expected," Martha said, looking down at the floor.

Jess and Nadia turned to each other, both cringing in embarrassment. Then Nadia's head snapped back around as though she'd just remembered something. She slapped Martha on the back, causing her to jolt forward in shock.

"Don't worry, today's going to be a great day. You'll see," Nadia said, giving Jess a wink.

"Nadia!" Jess nudged her friend and glared at her.

"You think so?" Martha said, her pale blue eyes looking almost pleadingly at Nadia as if they'd been starved of good news.

"Oh, just ignore her," Jess said as the bell started to ring.

They couldn't say more because it was time to line up and go into school.

"Good morning, girls, please take your seats," Miss Jennings said as they filed into the classroom in a silent line that now fragmented and dispersed as each girl moved towards their desk. "We won't be attending assembly straight away today. Mr Fothergill has asked that we begin with lessons."

A low groan spread around the room, from all except Jess and Nadia, who looked at each other in anticipation. Jess felt the hairs rise on the back of her neck. It was difficult to concentrate on any work, knowing what they were waiting for. Jess tried to imagine the important diplomatic and military leaders sitting around a table discussing terms and conditions, making a decision that would affect the world and its future.

At 10:30 the school bell rang. Nadia and Jess sat bolt upright and looked at Miss Jennings. Her expression was straight and serious, giving nothing away. Jess wondered if she knew what was to come. Miss Jennings stood, glanced at the girls and then left the classroom.

"Class, we are all to gather in the main hall," she said when she came back in, still straight-faced—the woman ought to have been a politician.

Nadia whipped her head around, her eyes searching for Jess. She nodded and mouthed, "This is it."

Jess nodded back, feeling the nervousness rise and whirl around in her stomach like butterflies emerging from their cocoons.

Filing into the hall in silence, each form took their usual places and waited for the Headteacher to join them. Mr Fothergill entered the room and stood before the pupils in silence. It was a long and stretched out silence that seemed never-ending and the air crackled with tension and unanswered questions.

"Students of Hickley School, I have an announcement from our Prime Minister, Mr David Lloyd George," Mr Fothergill said. There followed a wave of murmurs. Mr Fothergill raised his hand to command silence. "As of eleven o'clock this morning, the war will officially be at an end."

The whole school erupted in loud cheers.

Chapter 16

A Moment Of Joy Tinged With Sadness

All around them pupils hugged each other with tears of joy and relief flowing. A boy grabbed Nadia and started flinging her around the room. She let out a yelp, which turned to laughter, as the boy danced with her, round and round.

Jess smiled at the scene, before scanning the hall for Martha. She spotted her at the far end and made her way over, through the crowds of happy young people. Martha sat on the floor with her knees bent up to her chest. She had huge fat tears rolling down her face, forming wet patches on her skirt. Jess sat down next to her.

"It's all right, Martha," Jess said, putting an arm around her shoulders and pulling her closer. "Henry is going to be okay I promise." She took a deep breath, to steady her nerves while she waited for Martha to respond.

"But how can you be sure?" There was that look in Martha's round eyes again. Her face was even paler than normal, an unhealthy pallor, drained of all colour.

"I just know," said Jess, squeezing her hand. "I can't explain to you how I know, but you have to trust me."

Martha stared at Jess as if she could see right through her and into her soul.

"I hope you're right," she said, returning the squeeze. "There's something different about you, Jess. I can't say what it is. I feel like I know you, yet we'd never met before Friday. Strange, isn't it?" Martha smiled weakly through her tears.

Jess nodded back. She understood exactly what Martha was saying because she felt the same way.

"Come and join the celebrations," Jess said, standing up and offering her hand. "This is the best day ever."

Martha laughed as she stood to join her. "Best day ever," she said, mocking Jess. "You do come out with some funny things. I don't know where you get it from."

When a friend of Martha's came over and hugged her, Jess left them and went to find Nadia, who seemed relieved to be rescued from the happy commotion. The pair stood back from the celebrations, trying to take in the scene in front of them. Jess thought about all the children who wouldn't see their loved ones again and it tinged the moment of joy with sadness. So many lives were lost defending the country; men and young boys sent to the front line, never to return. It was all so real, but at the same time pointless. It seemed Mr Fothergill was aware of this too and once again, he raised his hand, signalling silence.

"At the hour of eleven, we will stand in silence to honour our fallen heroes. We know of ninety of our Old Boys who have lost their lives and we will make sure no one will ever forget them. Their names will be engraved on a memorial to remind pupils of the sacrifices they made and it will take pride of the place in this hall."

The pupils clapped and cheered. Jess looked towards where Mr Fothergill was pointing. It was at the entrance to the hall, in a prominent place for everyone to see. The memorial she'd looked at—the same one she presumed was in the foyer, where no one really took much notice of it.

I need to get this memorial put back where it belongs to remind everyone of the boys from this school who gave up their lives, Jess thought.

Mr Fothergill dismissed the pupils, saying they could take the rest of the day off. That was followed by more whoops of joy as the students streamed out of the school and into the streets.

When Jess and the others joined them, it looked as though everyone in the town had stopped work to celebrate. In the streets, people cheered, danced and sang.

"This is amazing!" Tomma said, grabbing Jess and twirling her around before she could object. This act of spontaneity was unusual for him. His face was alight, his eyes dancing with excitement and he was clearly swept up in the moment. Jess liked the feel of his strong hands holding hers. She smiled and twirled around some more.

*

As the time neared four o'clock, thoughts turned to going home.

"It feels like such a shame to leave," Nadia said, as they walked towards the coal house to collect their things. "Do you think we should try to come back again?"

"I don't think so," said Tomma. "This isn't our time, it's theirs. We should leave them to enjoy it."

Sensible Tomma was back again. Jess knew he was right, but was surprised at how sad she felt to leave. Amidst all the noise of the whistles, hoots and cheers, a silence descended on them as they set off back to the station.

It hadn't occurred to anyone what the declaration of a public holiday would mean for them, but when they arrived at the train station, they found out. All work had stopped for the day, including the running of the trains.

They were stuck in Hickley, 11th November 1918.

Chapter 17

An Unexpected Sleepover

"What do we do?" said Jess, beginning to feel frightened.

"I don't know," Nadia said, her face pale. She ran over to the station attendant. "Excuse me, are there no trains running at all tonight?"

"Only cargo ones, if they've got to get their business done as usual. Not everything can come to a halt. There is still technically a war on, you know."

"But no passenger trains to Kirkshaw?" Nadia said.

"I'm afraid not. There won't be another one now until four o'clock. tomorrow."

Nadia turned to face the others and took a deep breath. "Oh my God, this is awful. I never thought for one second we'd get stuck here. What if the magic doesn't work tomorrow and we can't get back at all?" she said.

"Don't say that, Nadia, I'm scared enough as it is. I want to go home." Jess thought she might cry. She looked at Tomma, hoping he might have an idea of what to do. Jess could tell by the set look of concentration on his face he was already thinking up a plan.

"We should camp in the station," Ash said. The girls

nodded, unable to speak. Ash turned to Tomma, looking for his response. "What do you say, mate?"

"Shush, I'm trying to think," Tomma said. "We're not supposed to be going home tonight, anyway are we?"

"Oh yeah, the sleepover!" Ash said.

"Exactly! So, if no one is expecting us, they aren't going to freak out when we don't show up, are they?"

"They will if we don't answer the register," Jess said. "They might ring our parents to find out why we're not there."

"That could be a problem," Tomma said, tapping on his bottom lip with his fingers. "Ah, but we were on the register here, right? Even though we don't live in this time. So as long as we go back to school, find a register and tick our names off, then sleep there tonight as if we're at the actual sleepover, no one will realise we're missing."

"That could work," Ash said, slapping Tomma on the back.

"Yeah, do you remember I said no one noticed whether we were there or not on Friday? They didn't have us down as absent though, they just failed to notice us," Nadia said.

"That might get us out of the sleepover, but it doesn't help us get out of here, does it?" Jess sighed, feeling frustrated and annoyed and wishing she'd never agreed to coming back.

"Let's worry about that tomorrow," said Tomma. "The trains will be back on, so with any luck, we can catch our one and get home."

There wasn't a lot else they could do and at least there was something safe and comforting about going back to Hickley School. It was a familiar place; one that seemed to accept them no matter what time zone they were in.

As they walked back up the hill, Jess scanned the crowds,

hoping to see Martha. Being drawn to Martha as she was, she knew seeing her friendly face again would make her feel much better, but she couldn't make her out in the crowds.

When they made it back up to Hickley School, the four children signed their names on the register in the office, leaving it open at that page, hoping it was enough to show they were present at the school. When they went back into the hall, they found Martha sitting alone at the back of the room looking so sad and lost, it almost broke Jess's heart. Jess raised her hand to the others to ask them to wait and she walked over to Martha, sitting down beside her.

"I thought you'd gone home," Martha said, looking up in surprise.

"Well, we did try," Jess said. "But there are no trains."

"Oh, yes, of course, the celebrations," Martha said, in a flat tone.

"You don't fancy joining in then?" Jess said.

"Not really."

Jess understood. Martha was too worried about her brother to want to celebrate. How could she be happy knowing he was still out on the frontline facing danger?

"Henry's going to be okay," Jess said.

"I know, you've said that already, but I wish I could be as positive as you. How has this war not worn you down?"

"It was terrible, it *is* terrible," Jess said, correcting herself. "Such tragic, pointless losses."

Martha sat up straight and turned to look at her. "You're different. I've never met anyone like you before."

Jess hesitated. "It's complicated... but we're not from around here and it looks as though we won't be able to get home tonight, so we're going to have to camp here. That's our excuse for coming back to school when everyone's been given a day off. What's yours?"

"It's quieter here, that's all," Martha said, staring around the empty hall.

"You want to camp out with us?" Jess said.

Martha looked horrified. "No! I can't do that. I have to go and collect Theresa and take her home. She goes to my neighbour's house after school, until I can pick her up. My mother and older sister, Elsie both work nights, so if I don't go home, Theresa will be on her own. You shouldn't stay here either. It's freezing. You can come to stay with me if you like."

"Really? What all of us?" Jess said.

"Why not? We have to look after each other, don't we?" she said. "Like I said, it's just Theresa and me tonight, so we have more than enough room."

Chapter 18

Martha's Guests

After discussing what to do and deciding they would rather stay in a warm house than be alone in a freezing-cold school hall, the children walked back through the still-crowded streets to Martha's house. The walk took around twenty minutes along back lanes, some of which were recognisable, even in the present day.

Martha led them down a dusty, cobbled road towards a mill that was billowing out thick black smoke. The windows were lit up in a golden yellow light that flickered and danced, casting shadows on the walls. Beyond it was a row of terrace cottages, stretching down to the far end of the street. Martha's house was the first one in the row. She opened the door and gestured for them to follow her in.

"You can put your things down in here," she said, pointing to the first room on the left. "Make yourselves comfortable. I'll just go and fetch Theresa."

Martha went out again as if in a hurry, leaving the four of them to take in the surroundings: their home for the evening.

"It's not much warmer in here, is it?" Ash said, rubbing his hands together and flapping his arms about.

"Hopefully Martha will be able to start a fire when she gets back," Nadia said as she surveyed the room.

It looked like a sitting room. There was an old worn sofa in the centre, facing a small open, cast-iron fireplace that had a big colourful rug in front of it. Behind the sofa was a dark wood dresser. Jess looked at the serious faces of the people staring back at her from the framed photos placed on there. She wondered which one of them was Henry.

"I guess this would be a good place to camp down for the night," Tomma said. "At least we won't be disturbing anyone if we're all in here."

Jess set her bag down, following Tomma's lead. Nadia and Ash did the same, then they all stood awkwardly, waiting for Martha to return.

Looking out of the bay window, they saw Martha walking past, holding hands with a little girl of around five years old, small and thin, with curly blonde hair. As the door clicked open, the sound of a smaller, lighter voice filtered through, alongside Martha's.

"I have some friends I'd like you to meet, Theresa. They are going to stay with us tonight. That will be nice, won't it? We don't get visitors very often, so we must be on our best behaviour."

On seeing them, Theresa seemed delighted to have new people to talk to. She asked question after question, whilst Martha set about trying to light the fire.

"Can I help?" Tomma said, kneeling beside her. His large frame making Martha seem tiny and frail in comparison, even though she was anything but.

"Oh no, I'm fine, it's just a little trickier to get the fire going when you don't have much coal to use. We have to ration it, see," Martha said. "I hope you have warm clothes with you or else you'll have to snuggle up together to keep warm tonight."

"Well, I don't mind that," Ash said, grinning widely.

Jess caught Tomma's eye and blushed. This wasn't exactly what her mother had in mind for the Big Sleepover.

"I don't have much to offer to eat either," Martha said. "I think I can make soup. There should be enough to go around."

"We'll help," Jess said, looking at Nadia, who nodded.

"Yes definitely. Just tell us what to do and we'll gladly do it," Nadia said.

"I'm hungry, Martha," Theresa moaned. She looked so tiny and skinny, in need of a decent meal. It didn't seem as though soup would be enough for her and Jess felt guilty for taking some of her share.

Martha gave her sister a hug. "It won't be long. Let me see if there is some bread left and you can have a little whilst the soup is heating. Come on."

She led Theresa, followed by Jess and Nadia, back into the narrow hall and into the next room. It was a small kitchen, in the centre of which was a wooden table. There was a large wrought iron oven set in an alcove on one side and, on the opposite wall, a dresser hung with cups and plates. Pots and pans hung down from the ceiling and Martha reached up to take the largest one. She set it down in the centre of the table.

Under Martha's instruction, the girls chopped vegetables and added them to the pan. Martha added some water, salt and herbs and then put it on the stove to boil.

"I'll light this and get the soup going, while you set up your things," she said.

*

Eating by candlelight whilst huddled together turned out to be not so bad after all. The six of them sat on the sleeping bags in front of the fire in the living room. The soup was bland but warming, and with a bit of stale bread to dip in it, it was filling enough. Jess made sure she gave extra to Theresa and, once the little girl had finished, her eyes were heavy with sleep. She curled up and snuggled beside Jess, who couldn't resist stroking her soft blond hair.

"I should get her to bed," Martha said.

"Where are your mum and sister?" Nadia asked, collecting together the bowls and plates.

"Mum's a nurse up at the hospital at the top of the hill, where my dad is recovering, and Elsie works at the mill just down the road here."

Jess remembered passing the mill on the way to Martha's house. Its tall chimneys spewing out black smoke right on their doorstep. She imagined all that smoke settling on the outsides of the houses, gradually turning the stone black. It couldn't be healthy to live so close to that, she thought.

"It's the reason we live here. Dad and Henry both work at the mill, but Henry's away, as you know, and Dad's recuperating from his injuries. Anyway, it's mostly women and girls who work there at the moment, except for the men who are too old or unable to fight. They make cloth, but during the war, it's been set up for sewing uniforms and all the other military things the soldiers need. They work day and night. My poor sister got unlucky with the night shifts because she's one of the younger ones who doesn't have the responsibilities of a family to look after. It's been left to me to care for Theresa while they're out."

"That's a lot of responsibility for you," Nadia said, who couldn't imagine anything worse.

"You get used to it," Martha said. "Besides, I don't have any other choice."

Martha picked up Theresa, who stirred and opened her eyes just a touch before the heavy lids dropped closed again. She smiled and muttered something before snuggling into Martha's chest.

"I think I will take to my bed too," Martha said, turning towards the others. "Please make this home your own for the evening. I hope you will be comfortable enough."

The children nodded and said their thanks, then watched as Martha carried her sister up the steep stairs.

"Martha's so sweet," Nadia said, closing the living room door to keep in the heat. "If it wasn't for her, we'd be in that freezing school hall on a cold and uncomfortable floor."

"I know, thank goodness she came to our rescue," Jess said.

Even though she would have preferred to be at home in her own bed, Jess felt safe at Martha's house and had the familiar feeling she'd already experienced. It was as though she knew Martha and her family somehow. She thought perhaps they'd met in a previous life if that was at all possible, but then, she was beginning to think anything was.

"It's freezing. I'm getting in here," Ash said, wriggling into his sleeping bag. "What shall we do? Girls on one side boys on the other? Or would you prefer to snuggle up together? I can keep you warm, eh, Nad?" Ash winked at Nadia, flashing his cheeky grin.

The girls ignored him, turning instead to their belongings.

The fire had burned down to nothing and the house was beginning to go cold, so the girls decided it would be warmer to sleep in their clothes rather than change into pyjamas. In the warmth of her sleeping bag, Jess struggled into her jeans and replaced her blouse with the jumper she'd brought from home. Once settled, she moved closer to Nadia for warmth. After several involuntary shivers, her eyes began to feel heavy and, to the sound of light snoring from all around her, she drifted off to sleep. She was woken—what seemed like minutes later—by a loud, piercing scream.

Chapter 19

Searching In The Darkness

Jess sat up, the shock of the scream setting all her senses on full alert. The room was in complete darkness and her eyes strained to adjust to their surroundings.

"Nadia, wake up," she said, nudging her friend. "Something's wrong."

"What?" Nadia said, in a moaning protest before turning over and snuggling deeper into her sleeping bag.

The sound of heavy steps rushing down the stairs caused the others to stir. Martha then burst into the room flinging the door open with such force it hit the wall.

Jess struggled out of her sleeping bag and jumped up. Martha held an oil lamp in her hand, which brought a soft light into the room. Jess could see Martha's long hair loose around her shoulders. It was as wild as her eyes.

"It's Theresa! She's gone."

Tomma jumped up to join Jess. He reached out to rest a hand on Martha's arm.

"What do you mean, gone?" he asked.

"What do you think I mean?" Martha snapped, pulling her arm from his reach with such force it caused the oil lamp to sway, sending swirling light around the living room.

"Have you checked the house? Could she have got up to use the toilet?" Tomma said. His voice was calm and authoritative, though Jess knew he would be feeling anything but.

"I'll go and check," Ash said, rushing out of the door. Jess could hear him running up the stairs as though he'd taken them three at a time. He came back down almost straight away.

"There's no bathroom up there. Just two bedrooms," he said, somewhat bewildered.

Martha huffed. "Who has a bathroom upstairs?" she said, her voice edgy with fear. "What do you think we are? Royalty?"

Ash looked embarrassed before a realisation hit him. "Bathroom outside?"

"Only a lavatory and she wouldn't go out there on her own at night. She's too scared."

"I'll go and check anyway," he said, dashing into the kitchen. A second later he shouted, "Back door's open."

Martha's eyes went wider as she pushed past Tomma, scrambling to get to the kitchen. "Is she out there?"

"Give me the lamp," Tomma said. "I'll go and see."

He strode off and Jess came towards Martha, putting her arms around her as they waited for Tomma and Ash to check around the garden. Jess tried to focus her eyes on the blackness outside but couldn't see beyond the outhouse, where the toilet was. The girls watched as the light from the oil lamp moved around the garden. Martha stood in silence, wringing her hands and fixing her gaze on the blackness.

"She's not out there," Tomma said, as he came running back up the path, with Ash behind him. Tomma paused, looking uncomfortable and a heavy silence surrounded them. "The back-gate is open though."

Tomma switched his gaze to Jess so she could see the concern reflected in his eyes. Jess gulped, trying to swallow the fear rising through her. Martha let out a soft wail.

"Could someone have taken her?" Jess said. "I don't understand. I never heard anything."

"Neither did I," Martha said. "I was sleeping and she was beside me. Then I woke up cold and realised she was no longer there. I don't understand it either."

Jess had never felt so alone and helpless. It didn't make sense that Theresa could just vanish into the night. The thought filled her with dread. She had no idea what they were dealing with, alone in a world they knew nothing about. They were only children themselves, but left in charge of a little girl, they had failed. Theresa was missing and no one knew what to do about it. This was a responsibility, it seemed, that was beyond them.

"We can go and look for her," Tomma said. "Where does the back-gate lead to?"

Martha was shaking and seemed paralysed with fear. "I can't lose her too. I can't, I can't," she said, in such a small voice, it was barely audible.

Jess looked at her new friend breaking with the pressure the war had put on her family. She didn't need this added strain. They had to help her.

"I know where it goes," Jess said, casting a reassuring look towards Martha. "One way goes back to the road and the other to the playing field. At least it did the last time I was down there. I've no idea what is there now, but I recognised this road when we walked here from school. My nan used to live on it." Jess clasped Martha's hand. "We'll split up and look for her. I'm sure she won't have gone far. Do you have any more lamps?"

Martha nodded as Nadia stepped forward and put her arms around her. "In the kitchen."

Tomma and Ash went to grab some more lamps whilst Nadia guided Martha towards her coat, sensing she needed help even with such an ordinary task. The fear of losing her little sister had caused Martha to turn helpless. Jess put on her coat and zipped it up tight. She took hold of the lamp Ash handed to her and gripped the cold metal handle as she stepped out into the darkness.

"Are you okay about doing this?" Tomma said quietly into Jess's ear. "You hate the dark."

"I know I do. You don't have to remind me! But I'm scared of pretty much everything and we have to find Theresa. It's freezing out here. Did you see how thin and pale she was? She won't last five minutes."

"What if she's been taken? She could be anywhere by now," Tomma said.

"I don't think she has," Jess said.

"What makes you so sure?"

"The way she just disappeared without any of us hearing a thing. If she was taken, there would have been a struggle."

"What?" Tomma said, coming to a halt and grabbing Jess by the shoulder to stop her too. "Do you think she just walked off then?" Tomma shook his head. "It doesn't make sense."

Jess looked back at the house. They were near the bottom of the garden now and Martha and Nadia were out of earshot.

"I think she might have been sleepwalking."

"Sleepwalking!"

"Shh," Jess said, pulling at his arm to move him even further down the garden and away from the house. "My mum used to do it when she was little. I'd forgotten all about it until now when I remembered her telling me how she walked out of the house one night across the road to the park. Her parents found her on the swings and she had no idea how she got there."

"That's so weird. You think Theresa might have done something similar?" Tomma said.

"It's possible," she said. "But if she hasn't and if someone did somehow take her then. . ." Jess looked at him. She didn't want to give in to her fears of what that might mean.

They stared at each other.

"I'll go this way to check the road around the mill," Ash said, catching up with them. "See if she's made it to the road."

"I'll take Martha and we'll look out front," Nadia shouted down, as she stood at the open back door.

Jess could see Martha was shaking and thought it was probably as much from fear as it was from being cold.

"We'll go this way," Tomma said, nodding towards the other side of the alleyway.

Jess gulped. It was pitch black and impossible to see more than just past your feet. The low light from the oil lamps cast an eerie shadow on the ground.

"Come on, I'll lead," Tomma said, taking her hand.

Stumbling their way down the dirt track, as though blindfolded, Jess and Tomma made it to the end without any sign of Theresa.

"This is where the playing field is," Jess said, as they emerged from the denseness of the wooded path into the open fields.

"There's a bit more than a playing field here now," Tomma said as they looked out over the vast expanse of blackness. "Where does it lead to? Do you know?"

"Well, it's a bit hard to work it out from memory and in the dark," Jess said. "I haven't been down here for ages, but there was a field just here and then an overgrown hedgerow surrounding it that led down to—"

She stopped. Tomma glanced at her.

"Led down to what, Jess?"

"The railway line," she said. "It's a disused one as I know it, but I bet it's not out of use in this time."

"The railway attendant said there might still be cargo trains running tonight," Tomma said.

Jess felt her heart drop into her stomach as panic washed through her.

"We better get down there just in case," she said.

The ground was hard with frost and both Jess and Tomma stumbled as they raced across the field towards the hedge. Scrabbling through the overgrown brambles, they managed to make their way down towards the railway track.

Chapter 20

A Near Miss

Jess held up her lamp, straining her eyes to see, but it was like looking through dirty water. Tomma was on the opposite side of the track and they searched around for any sign of the little girl but with every passing minute, Jess was beginning to think it was hopeless. The oil lamp provided hardly any light and she kept tripping up in the darkness, so she moved onto the track, hoping it might be easier if she walked along it, rather than at the side.

As she stood, holding up her lamp and looking for Tomma's light, Jess suddenly spotted a small black shape on the track some way ahead.

"Theresa!" she screamed, beginning to run, thoughts of bringing Theresa home safely to Martha the only thing on her mind.

Without concentrating on looking where she was going, Jess didn't notice one of the railway sleepers sticking up higher than the rest. She lurched forward and unable to stop herself, fell face first towards the ground. The oil lamp landing on the floor with a loud clatter, cutting out and plunging her into total darkness.

Jess groaned. The fall had knocked the wind out of her and, as she tried to move, found she was stuck. Somehow, her foot had become wedged underneath the railway sleeper. Her knee hurt too and when she touched it Jess felt a warm stickiness seeping through her jeans. She began to struggle to release her foot, but every move sent a sharp pain up her leg. She thought she might pass out.

"Help!" she shouted. "Tomma! Ash! Anybody! I'm stuck."

There was no response. Jess wondered how far away the others had spread in their desperate search. She struggled some more and then stopped as fear gripped her. There was a noise coming from behind that sounded very much like a train.

Jess tried to twist to see, but couldn't move without causing searing pain. She screamed again and wrestled desperately with her foot.

"Theresa!" Jess shouted. "Theresa, get up!"

Jess thought if she could get the little girl to move, she might be able to spare at least one of their lives. She began to cry in desperation. The train was getting closer and her heart was thumping so loudly. The noise echoed through her ears in time with the sound of the approaching train.

Jess realised she couldn't give in. She had to live. Fear turned to anger and in a last-ditch attempt, she used all her strength, channelling that anger as she yanked at her foot, no longer feeling, or caring about the pain. Finally, it loosened from under the broken sleeper and Jess managed to wrench free from the line. She flung herself to the side of the track just in time.

Relief flooded through her as the train rattled by, but it

was replaced by more fear as she bolted upright and looked beyond it to the small black shape in the distance.

"Jess, are you all right?" Ash said, rushing to her side.

Jess looked at the familiar face of her friend, as she struggled to get up.

"We need to get Theresa!" Jess said, by now hysterical as she began to scream out Theresa's name.

The train was getting closer and Theresa hadn't moved. The piercing whistle of the train echoed through the still night air, along with the screech of its brakes. It was a cargo train and wasn't travelling as fast as an ordinary passenger one, but the driver must have seen the obstruction and by the sound of the screeching brakes, was attempting to avoid a collision and bring the train to a stop. Ash held on to her as Jess buried her face in his shoulders, her body shuddering with uncontrollable sobs, unable to look up.

When the train continued on its journey, chugging steadily away, Jess and Ash stared at each other in surprise. Looking towards the train, they saw it had moved beyond where the crumpled body of Theresa had been lying, leaving nothing in its wake.

"He didn't stop," Jess cried in surprise. Fear gripped her once more. "Oh my God, did he drag over her body?" She tried to run but her leg was in so much pain, it was impossible.

"I've got her," they heard a voice cry out in the distance. It was Tomma.

In deep shock, neither Jess nor Ash could reply.

"Jess, talk to me—are you there?" Tomma's voice sounded desperate. "Please say something."

"I'm here with Ash," she shouted back. "Is Theresa safe?"

The words hung in the air as she said them, her breath held tight.

"She's alive," Tomma said. "Only just."

Jess gasped and turned to Ash.

"I'll go and help him," Ash said. He rushed towards the light of Tomma's lamp and Jess waited for a few anxious moments until she saw them reappear, walking back along the track towards her.

Tomma carried Theresa in his arms. When they reached her, Tomma gave Theresa to Ash and took off his coat to wrap around her. Then he turned to Jess.

"You're hurt," he said, noticing how she was stood with one leg suspended off the floor.

"I'm fine," she said, groaning with pain as she tried to put her foot down. "What happened?" She grabbed Tomma's arm so she could use him for support.

"I heard screams and tried to follow the sound but then I saw the train and realised Theresa was there. I pulled her away just in time."

Jess flung her arms around him. "Tomma, thank God you did! I thought she was going to be killed."

Tomma held her tight.

"We need to get her home. She's freezing," Ash said.

Quickly Jess pulled away from Tomma and attempted to walk on her own, but her knee and ankle hurt so much, she almost stumbled again before Tomma caught her. Then her eyes landed on Theresa and her pale little face, eyes closed.

"Oh God, please let her be okay," she said.

Tomma wrapped Theresa tighter still in his jacket as Ash

pulled her closer to his chest. Her tiny feet poked out from the end of the jacket.

"Oh, Theresa, what were you doing coming out here all alone?" Jess said, stroking her hair. Her hands moved to touch her feet. "Tomma she's freezing. Let me get my socks for her." Jess began to move but it was slow, painful and awkward. She winced.

"We haven't got time for that," Tomma said.

"Reach into my pockets and get out my gloves," Ash instructed. "They should cover her feet."

Jess did as he asked, tucking Theresa's gloved feet into the coat as much as possible before bending down to pick up the lamp.

"We should go this way," she said, pointing down the track. "If we follow the track it leads us to the road. It will be quicker to go back that way and easier than carrying her through all that bramble and across the fields."

Ash set off ahead and ignoring the searing pain, Jess held on to Tomma. His arm was wrapped around her waist, holding her up. He stopped and turned to face her, pulling her close in a tight hug.

"I don't know what I would have done if anything had happened to you," he said into her ear.

Jess held on tightly to him. They stayed there for a few seconds until she gently pulled away.

"Come on, we need to get back," she said softly.

Moving as quickly as she could, Jess tried to focus on getting Theresa home to warmth and safety. She prayed they wouldn't be too late.

Chapter 21

No Good Nurses?

When they arrived back at Martha's house, Jess could see Martha and Nadia in the front room, illuminated by the soft lighting from the oil lamps. On spotting them, the girls rushed out to let them in. Jess felt the warmth of the house envelope her as she stepped inside. Ash took Theresa straight into the living room and laid her down on his sleeping bag in front of the fire, now roaring away once more. Then he dashed out of the room and Jess could hear the thundering of his heavy boots going up the stairs.

Martha collapsed in front of her sister, tears streaming down her face. "My poor baby sister, what happened to you?"

"We found her down by the railway line," Tomma said. "Jess thinks she may have been sleepwalking."

"Sleepwalking!" Martha shook her head in disbelief and leaned over to give Theresa a light kiss on the forehead. "She's freezing cold." She gently picked her up and held her close to her chest.

Ash came charging down the stairs and into the living room. "Blankets," he said, dumping them on the floor.

Nadia grabbed one and wrapped it around Theresa's little frame. "What can we do to help?"

"Boil some water to make some tea," Martha said, through sobs. "We need to make her warm again."

Martha rocked Theresa back and forth as she sat on the floor in front of the fire, singing a lullaby in a soft voice. She stayed like that until Nadia returned with the drink.

"I didn't know what to put it in, so I hope this will do," she said, handing an enamel mug to Martha.

Martha pulled Theresa up to a sitting position and carefully dripped some of the warm liquid on to her lips. After a few attempts, Theresa began to cough and for the first time, opened her eyes. She looked all around her, not registering where she was or why everyone was staring at her.

"Martha?" she said in a tiny voice. "Why are you crying? Is it Papa?"

"Sweet little sister," Martha said, choking on both laughter and tears. "Have you really no idea what you have just put us all through?"

Theresa's confused face had everyone laughing. The sense of relief so strong it made the moment seem much funnier than it was.

"I don't know what Mama will say about this when she comes home," Martha said, as she turned away from Theresa, lowering her voice and becoming serious once more. "Theresa could have died and if—" She choked on the words. "If you hadn't been here, I don't know what I would have done."

Martha wiped the tears from her eyes with her nightshirt sleeve and looked at her sister, smoothing a hand across

Theresa's cheek. "I think we should lock the doors from now on, don't you?"

*

As a chink of daylight filtered in through the thick material of the lounge curtains, Jess heard the front door slam and the sound of voices. Her ears followed the noise of the chatting as it moved to the other side of the lounge wall, into the kitchen. She sat up, feeling stiff and sore all over.

Wincing as she pulled her legs out of the sleeping bag, Jess realised she hadn't even washed the wound on her knee. The material of her jeans was integrated into the newly formed scab and it was going to hurt to prise them apart.

The others around her stirred and began to sit up one at a time.

"Urgh, I'm shattered," Ash said. "That was like the most stressful night ever, and I hardly got any sleep, being on the floor."

"Aww, poor Ash. You're used to sleeping on luxury sprung mattresses with silk sheets, are you?" Nadia said, sticking out her bottom lip as she looked at him.

"Ha, you got me. I'm no boy scout, that's for sure," he said. "But neither are you, to be fair."

"No, that's true. But strangely, I slept like a log. After everything that happened last night, I think I just passed out," Nadia said.

Tomma was looking at Jess's knee and frowning. "You're going to have to get that sorted out when we get home," he said. "I doubt they'll be able to do much here."

"Isn't Martha's mum a nurse?" Nadia said.

"Yeah, but she's a nurse in 1918. They can't have been that good back then, can they?" Tomma said.

"Who said nurses in 1918 are no good, then?" a voice boomed. "And who the devil are you? Should I be sending for the police right now?"

Chapter 22

Saying Goodbye

The children froze as they realised Martha's mum was standing at the door with an older girl, who must have been Martha's sister. They each turned to look her way, offering a sheepish smile.

Tomma stood first and walked towards her offering his hand for her to shake. She looked a little surprised and amused, but took it anyway.

"Mrs Stenchion, sorry, my name is Tomma Handley. These are my friends: Ash Mundair, Jess Chadwick and Nadia Kaminski." He pointed to the others as he spoke. "We're friends of Martha's and we had a bit of trouble getting home yesterday, what with the trains being cancelled and everything, so Martha offered to put us up here."

"Yes, we're really sorry to take up your living room. We'll be out of your way as soon as possible. We don't want to be any trouble," Jess said.

"That's quite all right. You gave me a shock, that's all. Now, what is this you've done to your knee, young lady?"

Jess cringed and felt her face burning. She tried to stand up straighter but the pain was too great. "I had a fall last night," she said, looking down at the floor.

"Last night? What were you doing to injure yourself so badly?" Mrs Stenchion asked.

"It's a long story," Jess said.

"And one that you might need to sit down to hear, Mama," Martha said, as she appeared behind her mother. Martha looked close to tears again.

"My dear, whatever is the matter? You look awful," Mrs Stenchion said. She took her daughter in her arms and led her to the sofa. Martha sat down and told her all about the previous evening. Jess watched as Martha's mum grew pale.

"I'm alright though Mama," Theresa said, running into the living room and throwing her arms around her mother. She was dressed now and her cheeks had some colour back in them. Her blond curls were tied back in a half ponytail, the loose ends trailing across her shoulders like a golden mane.

"Thank the Lord," Mrs Stenchion said, enveloping Theresa in her arms and kissing the top of her head. Then she pulled away and began turning her daughter this way and that to examine her. Theresa smiled at Martha and went to sit on her knee.

Jess felt like they were intruding on a private moment. She nudged Nadia and whispered in her ear. "We should go."

The girls started to pack away their things. Jess wincing as she tried to put weight on her foot. The boys took the hint and began putting on their coats too until Mrs Stenchion raised her hand to stop them.

"Where do you think you are going?" she asked.

Mouths opened and closed as the children stared at each

other, before turning back towards Martha and her family. Martha put a hand over her mouth to stifle a giggle.

"You're not going anywhere until I've taken a look at your ankle and that wound on your knee and I haven't even had a chance to thank you all for saving my daughter. Come into the kitchen where it's warm. I've some eggs old Nancy at the hospital gave me. I'm sure you're all hungry, aren't you?"

The children put down their things, their expressions softening, as they relaxed. They followed Mrs Stenchion into the kitchen and Jess was leaning once again on Tomma for support.

"It was Jess who realised Theresa must have been sleep-walking," Tomma said, looking proudly at her. "We might not have found her in time if she hadn't."

Jess raised her eyebrows and shook her head as Tomma looked at her with a goofy smile on his face. She wished he'd not put her on the spot like that. It was so embarrassing.

"It was such quick thinking, Jess. We're so grateful to you," Mrs Stenchion said.

"She said her mum used to do the same when she was little," Tomma said.

"Oh, I see. Who is your mother. Would I know her?"

Tomma's mouth snapped shut and he looked at the floor as Jess glared at him.

"Probably not. We're not from here, but we're living in Kirkshaw at the moment," Jess said, finding the confidence to speak up for once. "We really should get back to the station as soon as we can. We couldn't get home yesterday because there were no trains and our parents will probably be worrying about us."

"Yes, of course, we mustn't keep you. Please allow me to feed you first before you get on your way. It's the least I can do. Plus, I have a pair of crutches in the out-house. You are welcome to take those too. I'm sure you will need them."

After toast, eggs and cups of weak, sugary tea, the children picked up their things ready to leave. They said goodbye to Theresa, Mrs Stenchion and Martha's older sister, Elsie. Martha decided to walk them to the end of the road. Jess couldn't help but give an extra-long cuddle to Theresa, saying her own little silent prayer that she was safe and well. Ash made Theresa laugh by tickling her. Having a younger sister of a similar age, he was used to dealing with little ones.

"There won't be any school today, because of the big announcement yesterday. You do know there is only one train a day to Kirkshaw don't you?" Martha said.

"Yeah, we found that out yesterday," Nadia said. "But don't worry about us. We'll just hang out at the station and chill."

Martha looked at Nadia as though she was speaking in a foreign language.

"Yes, it is very chilly, so you should keep wrapped up, but don't hurt yourself by doing anything silly. Hanging isn't recommended you know," Martha said.

The children laughed.

"What?"

"Oh, nothing, just ignore us," Jess said, stopping to rest on the wooden crutches and turning to Martha. "Thank you so much for looking out for us and giving us a place to stay. We really would have been lost without you. It's been so lovely meeting you." She could feel her eyes burning as they filled with hot tears.

"You're not coming back, are you?" Martha said.

"I'm afraid not," Jess said sadly. "And I'll miss you."

"I'll miss you too," Martha said, hugging Jess.

Jess tried to breathe through the urge to cry. She waved at Martha before she set off with her friends towards the station, albeit at a slow pace in order for her to keep up with them.

"What a strange couple of days this has been," Nadia said. "I can't wait to go home and have a shower and do my hair. I feel disgusting."

"You don't look it," Ash said, with a wink.

"Yeah? Well, I feel it and that's all that counts."

"Nadia, you're so funny," Jess said.

"You don't know what it's like having hair that can't make up its mind if it wants to be curly or straight and ends up being a big frizzy mess instead."

"I love your hair," Jess said warmly. "I'd swap it for this any day." She pulled at the ends of her auburn locks.

"Your hair is gorgeous. It's just like Martha's," Nadia said.

"No, it is not!"

"It is!" Nadia, Ash and Tomma said at the same time.

Jess thought about Martha and her lovely family and thought she might start to cry again. She hobbled along in silence.

"Do you think we'll get into trouble when we get home?" Jess said after a while.

"Your guess is as good as mine," said Tomma. "We have to get home first though."

Chapter 23

Did You Miss Me?

The station guard they had met the previous day was back on duty, and when she confirmed the train to Kirkshaw was operating and would be leaving at four o'clock, she was met with a cheer all around. Clearly confused, but too polite to ask, she merely smiled at the children and asked if they wanted to sit in the waiting room by the fire. Glad of the warmth, they agreed.

With no money to buy any food, the children were hungry as well as cold. It was going to be a long day. The station guard must have felt sorry for them because when she returned from her lunch break, she made them all a cup of tea.

"I don't think I've ever drunk so much tea," Nadia said with a giggle.

*

The station was strangely deserted and when the train arrived, they made their way automatically to the end of the platform, getting on the last carriage. They settled down for the journey, hoping they had done everything they needed in order to make it home.

"I'll kind of miss this train," Nadia said. "We aren't doing this again, right?"

"No way," Tomma said.

"Absolutely not," Jess said, shaking her head.

"No!" Ash yelled.

The reply was unanimous and it made Nadia chuckle.

"I know what you mean, though," Tomma said. "It's kind of cool travelling like this and being able to sit down for the journey for once."

"Not standing under someone's stinky armpit, you mean," Nadia said, curling her nose.

Ash jumped up. "Yeah and being able to stick your head out of the window like this."

"Ash! Stop it," Jess grabbed his coat and pulled him back.

Ash was laughing but she was not impressed. "Just teasing, Jessie." He ruffled her hair.

"Well, I don't think it's funny," Jess said, smoothing down her hair then folding her arms across her chest.

"Think someone's tired and grumpy," Ash said as if he was talking to a toddler.

Jess stuck her tongue out at him.

"Of course she is, Ash, we all are. Leave her alone you big bully," Nadia said.

Ash sat back down on the bench next to Nadia and opposite Tomma, who moved closer to Jess and put his arm around her. Nadia raised her eyebrows, but Jess ignored her and rested her head on Tomma's shoulders. The gentle rocking of the train was making her sleepy and she was so tired it was a struggle to stay awake. She felt herself drifting off. . .

"Jess, Jess! We're back, look!"

With Tomma's voice in her ear and a gentle nudging as he moved the shoulder she was resting on, Jess sat up and cracked open her eyes to see Kirkshaw station just coming into view.

"Oh, how I love that dirty, fallen-down old shack," Jess said, standing up and adjusting her crutches under her armpits.

She reached for her bag but it was impossible to bend down to pick it up when you had two wooden sticks under each arm. Ash laughed at the scene but picked it up for her.

They stepped off the train and onto the platform and Ash got down on his knees and kissed the ground, much to the confusion of the other passengers around them. The girls giggled.

"Home at last," Ash declared. "Now to find out if we're grounded for the rest of our lives. Just in case, I want to say that it's been great knowing you."

Jess hugged Nadia, said goodbye to Ash and was about to do the same to Tomma.

"I'm going to walk Jess home," Tomma said to the others. "I'll catch you later."

Jess looked at him in surprise but feeling grateful at the same time. She wasn't sure she would have been able to manage to hobble home on her own whilst carrying a huge rucksack. Although Mrs Stenchion had bandaged up her knee and ankle, both were sore and painful when she walked. She was also dreading going home in case her mother was freaking out about them skipping school.

"What? You didn't think I was going to leave you to get home by yourself in that state, did you?" he said, looking down at her wounds.

Nadia winked at Jess and turned to leave with Ash.

By the time they got to Jess's house, her mum was just pulling into the drive. Jess took a deep breath and steadied herself against the crutches. She gave Tomma a nervous sideways glance as Jess's mum got out of the car.

Her mum looked her up and down, and spotting the bandages and crutches straight away, came rushing over with a worried look on her face.

"Oh my goodness, what did you do?" she said, about to grab on to Jess's arm, but at the last minute she changed her mind. She opened the door, gesturing for Jess and Tomma to go inside. They walked ahead of her, in towards the kitchen.

Jess looked at Tomma who nodded reassuringly.

"Jess had a bit of an accident," Tomma said. His face coloured in embarrassment.

"What sort of an accident and why didn't the school ring me?" her mum demanded.

Jess hobbled towards the table and Tomma helped her sit down, propping her leg up on another chair.

"She fell," he said. "We were all playing outside and it got a bit messy."

"But I told them I was fine and they didn't need to worry you about it," Jess said.

"Oh Jess, how did you manage to get yourself in this state though? Does it hurt much?"

"A bit," Jess said. "Only when I stand and try to walk. It's better when I can sit."

"Do I take it the sleepover was a success then, judging by the state of the both of you?" Her mum got up and went over to the sink to fill the kettle. "Would either of you like a cuppa?"

Jess and Tomma looked at each other and smiled.

So far, so good, Jess thought.

They'd arrived home at the usual time and her mother hadn't missed her at all. The school couldn't have reported them absent from the sleepover, otherwise, she would have been called about it.

"Do you know what, Mum, I'm a bit fed up of tea. Do we have anything more. . . modern?"

"Well, we have some Diet Coke in the fridge, will that do?"

Chapter 24

Connecting With The Past

The next day, Jess was at the station early again, after getting a lift from her mum. The novelty of walking around on crutches had long worn off. It was hard work and she couldn't wait for her ankle to heal so she could walk on it properly again. She sat on a bench out the front of the station, waiting for the others to arrive.

"Shall we even look to see if there's an old carriage at the end?" Nadia asked.

"You can look, I suppose," Jess said. "But there's no way we're getting on it! Anyway, we didn't have a power cut or anything this morning, did we? There's nothing strange about the day."

"Yeah, but I'm gonna look anyway," Nadia said.

When the train arrived, it was packed with commuters from end to end. There was no old-fashioned carriage at the back and it was standing room only. It wasn't as if that should have surprised them. They hadn't summoned the steam train before. It was as though the train had chosen to appear so they could get on it and travel back in time.

"There's your answer, then," Tomma said, as he helped Jess on to the train.

Jess had never been so glad to be on an over-crowded train, even if it did mean getting squashed. She was relieved when someone offered up their seat. Standing on one leg was tiring, even if she did have crutches to lean on.

When the train arrived at Hickley station, a swarm of school children and commuters got off, dispersing in different directions. The children let the rush die down, not able to go too fast anyway because of Jess. They made their way outside to the road, which was busy with the morning rush-hour traffic.

"We're back baby," Ash said, turning full circle with his arms spread out. He whooped loudly, causing others to turn and stare at him. Not that Ash cared. He wasn't particularly bothered about what other people thought of him.

The noise of the cars and buses and the thrum of people in the streets was almost too much for Jess. She missed the calm of 1918, even though it smelled of horses and factory pollution. She struggled up the hill to school on her crutches, Tomma and Nadia by her side.

Hickley School was a familiar mix of old and new buildings. The children looked at each other and grinned.

"Seems weird to see it like this again," said Tomma.

"Just think—heating, hot food at lunchtime, and we can all be in the same class again," Ash said.

"And no more disgusting uniforms," Nadia shuddered. She'd put the uniform safely away in her wardrobe. It was the only physical thing left to remind her of what they had experienced, but she wasn't about to put it on again any time soon.

At registration, they greeted their classmates as though they hadn't seen them in months.

"It's so good to see you," Jess said to her form teacher, Mr Ward, much to his surprise.

*

Their first lesson was history. All four of them were back in the same class once more.

"Right everyone," Mrs Kennedy said, once they were settled with their books in front of them. "We've covered the Victorian era from 1898 when our school first opened. Now we're moving on to the First World War, 1914 to 1918. How was Hickley affected?"

Tomma and Ash, who were sitting in front of Jess and Nadia, turned around to face them. Both raised their eyebrows and Ash mouthed, "What?" with a shocked expression on his face.

"This may surprise you to know, but Britain was subjected to bombing raids in World War I, but none that affected this area. Hull was bombed though and the east coast, near Great Yarmouth, but it was mainly London and Kent that took the hits. Even so, all the towns across the country felt the effects of war, as most of its young men volunteered their services and many died protecting their country. I would like you to do an assignment about some aspect of life during this time. I would like you to find out about any members of your family who were involved in the war," Mrs Kennedy said.

"You'll be going back as far as your great-grandparents, so if you have grandparents, it would be a good idea to ask them what they can remember."

Jess and Nadia looked at each other in amazement. *Was*

that why the train had taken them back to 1918? Was it to help them understand a major historical event they were now going to study in school?

Jess thought how lucky they were to have seen a small part of it for themselves.

*

"Mum, do you know if we have any relatives who fought in the First World War?" Jess asked at dinner that night.

"Oh, I'm not sure, to be honest. I think my grandma, your great-grandmother, had a brother who fought in it. You'd have to ask your nanna. Why's that?"

"We're doing a project at school and they asked us to find out. Do you know his name, this brother?" Jess said.

"No, I don't, sorry. I only know the surname, as it was Grandma's maiden name."

"And that was. . .?" Jess said, beginning to feel frustrated at her mum's vagueness.

"Stenchion. Funny name, isn't it?" her mum said.

"Stenchion?"

"Yep."

"Mum, what was my great-grandmother's first name?" Jess said, begin to feel her heart speed up.

Her mum looked as though she was conjuring up an image in her head. She smiled.

"Theresa," she said. "She was so lovely. Such a cuddly nan. She used to look after us when we were little kids. I miss her."

Jess felt all the blood rush out of her face as her mother

chatted. Stenchion was Martha's surname too and Theresa was Martha's little sister. The same little sister whose life they had saved.

Now Jess knew the real reason they had gone back in time to 1918. It was because of her. Theresa was her great grandmother and Jess had helped save her life. If Theresa had died, Jess wouldn't have existed at all.

Chapter 25

We Will Remember Them

Jess wrote her project about the lives of the people on the home front. She wrote about how women of all ages took over the jobs of the men, embracing their roles and doing as good a job, if not better. She wrote about how the mills of the area, famous for producing cloth and woollen goods, kept the soldiers in uniform throughout the war.

She wrote about the suffering of the people as they struggled to survive on rations, living with the stress of not knowing if their loved ones would survive. The Hickley Old Boys who represented not only the school, but the town itself, and lost their lives in the process. Jess wanted people to know their names, so she researched each of them, including some of their biographies in her project, along with a reminder of how important it was to remember these were real people, not just names on a board.

She also included some history of the school during the wartime and how the Head had been proud of the Old Boys, dedicating the memorial in their name and giving it pride of place in the school hall.

She put her heart and soul into her essay, feeling her

connection with Martha and Theresa with every word she wrote. The words flowed easily as if it were a story that wanted to be told and she was the person chosen to tell it.

*

A few weeks later when Jess and Nadia were walking through the main hall, Jess smiled to herself as they stopped in front of the war memorial.

"I'm so pleased they decided to move this back to its rightful place," she said to Nadia.

"Yes, I know, and it's thanks to you and that history essay of yours, Jess."

"We owed it to them though, didn't we?" Jess said, modestly playing down the praise.

The girls stared in silence at the memorial, eyes moving over the names, lost in their thoughts. Jess thought about Theresa and how if they hadn't gone back in time and saved her, she perhaps wouldn't have been standing there at that moment. It was a strange thought; one that made her shiver and the hairs on the back of her neck stand on end.

She turned, feeling as though someone was watching her, and her eyes scanned the room. It was crowded with pupils making their way through the hall to and from lunch, but Jess's eyes fixed on a familiar face staring back at her.

"Thank you," the girl mouthed, before turning and disappearing into the crowd.

Jess stood on tiptoes and strained her neck to see her, but she had gone.

About the Author

Nikki Young is a children's fiction author and writing tutor. She lives in Kent with her husband, three children and their Boston Terrier dog and is the author of 'The Mystery of the Disappearing Underpants' and the 'Time School' Series.

On a mission to get children writing, Nikki runs Storymakers, a creative writing club for children aged 7 and above, which provides weekly writing groups, holiday workshops and 1:1 tuition and mentoring.

Find out more at www.nikkiyoung.co.uk
Follow her on Twitter: @nikki_cyoung
Instagram: @nikkiyoungwriter
Facebook.com/nikkiyoungwriter

Printed in Great Britain
by Amazon